WAR'S LOST LOVE FOUND

An enduring story of
love, mystery, and miracles

Don J. Gaddo and Demaris H. Parks

Palmaya Publishing, North Carolina

WAR'S LOST LOVE FOUND

ISBN: 0-9707087-1-8

Library of Congress Control Number: 2002090345

Published by:
Palmaya Publishing
Box 773
Chapel Hill, North Carolina 27514

Printed in the United States by:
Morris Publishing
3212 East Highway 30
Kearney, NE 68847

THIS BOOK IS DEDICATED TO:

SUE ANDERSON-SMERLING
MY LITERARY ANGEL

AND

COLONEL HAROLD WEEKLEY
THE LAST OF THE B-17 DRIVERS
AN AMERICAN HERO
AND MOST IMPORTANTLY
MY FRIEND

A SPECIAL THANKS TO ROGER JAYNES
AN AUTHOR AND MENTOR

APPRECIATION TO:

- Vickie Speek and Tom Tock for their continuous support and encouragement.
- Bill and Peg Chase. The World War II memories they shared with me were a shining tribute to the words **duty. . honor. . country**.
- EAA AirVenture Oshkosh. The event that reminds all Americans that American patriotism is alive and well.
- Laura Schabinger for her interest in World War II.
- Allen Ostrom, a member of the 398th Bomb Group.
- Cheerleaders Lee Law and Missy Hagan.
- Henry and Marilyn, Jim and Nadine, Wally and Amber **for everything**.
- Sharon Gaddo for hours of hard work, encouragement, and loyalty.

WAR'S LOST LOVE FOUND

ALBERT JOSEPH HOWARD

LONDON, ENGLAND
SEPTEMBER 29, 2000

My father, Joseph Earl Howard, was a captain in the Royal Air Force. He was the pilot of a Jaguar GR1B Fighter Bomber. In many ways he followed the footsteps of my grandfather, Second Lieutenant Joseph Doglio, a World War II navigator in the United States Army Air Force. My grandfather was a member of the 398th Bomb Group stationed in Nuthampstead, England during the war.

* * * * *

My father, from the day I was old enough to understand the spoken word, told me it would be my responsibility to write the story of our family. "For the entire world to read," was the way he said it.

* * * * *

The story of our family is a drama of epic proportions. Those were my father's words, and to him, indeed it was. It is an intriguing story of mystery and unanswered questions. This is a story of a World War II romance and a love affair between two young and innocent people. A love affair that has endured the passage of time. Our story begins during the ravages of World War II, and now, as I write these words, the story continues.

* * * * *

I have examined the mysteries of our family. I have learned much and yet, even today, so many questions remain unanswered. The devoted love of two people, after an acquaintance of only four and one-half days, was so strong that I cannot comprehend its meaning. I cannot comprehend the effect that this enduring love, between my grandmother and my grandfather, had on our lives. I no longer try to understand this undying love, instead I embrace it for its compassion, its emotion and the life long affects this enduring love had on my grandmother, Anne Howard.

* * * * *

In reality this is her story. The story of Anne Howard, a saint of a woman. It is the story of her love affair with my grandfather who was killed in action over Germany on July 19, 1944. Yes, it is also the story of my father, a loving husband, a kind and generous father, but most of all, an understanding and faithful son.

* * * * *

My father would be disappointed that it is not I who write this book but instead I have given this responsibility to new friends. I am not a writer, but you see, I too have followed the tradition of my grandfather, Joseph David Doglio, and my father, Joseph Earl Howard. I have become a pilot in the Royal Air Force. The sky has become a member of our family. The sky seems to tug at our soul and the heavens tug at our heart. We don't seem fulfilled until we reach the war ravaged skies that once were owned by my grandfather, the navigator of a B-17 Flying Fortress named *Angel*. Maybe it is he who calls us to our duty, to our predetermined destiny. Perhaps it is his voice I hear as I reach the limitless blue horizons of those heavenly skies.

"Higher. That's it. Soar like an Eagle," the voice beckons.

"Is it you, grandfather?" I ask this question as I

seek a new cloud and a new corridor to the unknown and uncharted skies of the blue heavens.

But perhaps it is my father who speaks to me. His spirit and determination seem to be my inspiration and my constant companion. He, as my grandmother shaped his life, has shaped my life. He was both my grandmother and my grandfather and I, Albert Joseph Howard, have become the three of them. I feel their presence in all I do.

* * * * *

So now, read our story. Although written by new friends and yes, family, these words continue to intrigue me, now, more than ever.

* * * * *

This introduction is my only participation in this book. This is my family's epic tale of mystery, faith, eternal love, and unexplained miracles.

* * * * *

Believe, and imagine, for a belief in what awaits us is the eternal hope of a troubled world. To believe is to understand and to understand brings us closer to the mysteries that await us.

THE DIARY OF JOSEPH DOGLIO

OCTOBER 17, 1942
SOUTH WILMINGTON, ILLINOIS

Mom and dad agreed to my enlistment today. If all goes well I will enlist on November 2, just nine days before my twentieth birthday.

Mom is saddened by my decision. I see the pain in her eyes. More so I see her anguish by the way she moves. Her every move seems to torment her body. I tried to remove her fears. She smiles and tells me she understands. I know, at least I think I know, how she must feel.

Dad, well. Dad served in World War I. I guess he feels my pride in enlisting. Perhaps there is honor in my decision. I feel this sense of foreboding but deep down I know I have done the right thing.

NOVEMBER 1, 1942

SOUTH WILMINGTON, ILLINOIS

Mom had a surprise party for me today. I guess it

was both a birthday party and a going away party. So many people came by the house. I think every family in town stopped by. Some stayed for over an hour.

What is so amazing is that many of dad's coal mining friends dropped by before going to the mine. Their gesture of respect must have made dad feel good.

I popped into the kitchen to look in on mom. I hesitated before entering. Mom was sitting on a kitchen chair, by herself, just staring at the floor. She was crying. I know this must sound funny, but I cried too. I made sure she didn't see me. I don't think I'll ever forget the look on her face. So sullen and somber. But the more I think of it, I think it was a mother's face that in reality is full of love for a child that has always been in reach of her hand or in view of her smile. Wiping my tears, I joined my brother who, by heaven, was telling everyone I would be an Air Force hero. How embarrassing.

NOVEMBER 2, 1942
SOUTH WILMINGTON, ILLINOIS

8:30 AM. For all I know it could be midnight. None of us slept last night. Mom cried all night. Dad did his best to comfort her. His consoling and reassurances did little to ease her fears.

I don't know what time it was, maybe 2 AM. I heard her sobbing voice proclaim, "What if he doesn't come home? Albert, what if our son doesn't come home?" My stomach ached. My heart ached. I trembled inside. What if I don't come back? What does fate have in store for me?

Brother Junior came in. He sat on my bed. "Are you awake?" he asked.

I nodded. My window, as usual, was cracked about eight inches. The winter wind seemed more brisk on this night. The weather barrier plywood seemed defenseless against the cold wintry gusts of the north wind. The wintry wind caused the model of my B-17 Flying Fortress, hanging from my bedroom ceiling, to twist and turn as if it wanted to be set free from its long and narrow string shackles. The Fortress wanted to fly. To suddenly become real. The Fortress was my dream. The B-17 was why I chose the Air Force. I want to fly her, to be a part of a gallant crew, to bomb the Germans into submission. Well, I want to shorten the war and the B-17 would be my chariot. Oh God, it is so beautiful.

"Junior, what are you doing awake?"

"Joey, don't you think you should go and hold mama? She's been crying all night. You should. She needs you."

And so I did.

And at the moment I entered my parent's room the emotion overcame us. There were tears of agony, tears of anxiety, and there was this tinge of fear. Mom's tears held a sadness that only a mother can understand. There was sorrow in her eyes and yet as she clasped my neck she managed to stop crying. Then, as suddenly as the tears had stopped, they began again. Somehow she managed to find an uncommon strength. At that moment she gained a mother's courage. For a brief second she was fearless, full of fortitude. Suddenly she came to life with the heart of a lion. Her voice rose with a resolute tenacity as she hugged my neck with all the strength she could muster.

"Be brave, son. Do you hear me? Be brave."

Tears again. She paused and implored me "You come home, Joseph." The rest of her words were inaudible. Then we cried. Even Junior.

Now, in thirty minutes, I must leave for Great Lakes Naval Center. I'll sign in, be processed, and I will learn where I will be sent for basic training.

As this may be my last entry in my diary, at least for a while, I'll close by saying I dread saying goodbye. Somehow mom managed an egg and sausage breakfast. Heaven knows where she found the sausage. The eggs, I know, came from Uncle Joe.

Oh God, mom, I love you. Dad, I'll miss you and Junior . . . And Junior be strong for both of them.

* * * * *

They stood in front of the house as we pulled away. I couldn't take my eyes off them. Mom was wearing her flowered house dress. Her favorite apron was flopping in the cold November wind. Dad, in his heavy coat, boots buckled, was dressed as if he was on his way to Mr. Densmore's coal mine. And Junior, he didn't think I could see him as he hid behind the evergreen in front of the house. He didn't want me to see him cry.

Mom seemed calm. She bit her lip as I waved goodbye. Dad just stood there holding mom's hand.

Then we turned the corner. They were gone.

* * * * *

Mom and dad were no longer visible to my eyes. They would, however, remain in my heart for all the days of my life. In reality, they would never be gone.

POINT OF INTEREST

JULY 8, 2001
NORTH CAROLINA

Joseph's diary contains few entries for the 1943 calender year. I would suspect his training and everyday duties occupied the majority of his time.

Several of his entries are written on the following pages. Included are two letters Joseph mailed to his parents.

* * * * *

LETTER TO JOSEPH'S PARENTS

APRIL 2, 1943

DALHART, TEXAS

Dear Mom and Dad:

Sunday again – boy how those weeks are passing by. Just returned from church. Went to 8:15 mass. Woke up at seven this morning.

We changed into our summer uniforms yesterday. It's okay during the day, but it does get chilly at night with these sun tanned clothes on.

I had KP yesterday. But KP is fun. I was a waiter on two tables and after the dinner meal, when I went to the tables to cleanup, I found $.65 in a bowl. The boys had left me a tip. We finished up at 7:30 last night.

I hear that we might be classified next week. Sure hope so. I am getting tired of waiting. The boy that came with me from Lincoln was told he didn't pass. Well, he has been shipped out already.

I cracked the crystal on my watch yesterday so I brought it to the jewelers on the base here and he is going to put an unbreakable crystal in it's place. I'll get the watch back on Wednesday.

I received a letter from Aunt Pauline and she sent me two dollars. That was swell.

We go on parade at 3:00 o'clock today. We have parade every Sunday.

Well, hope everything is okay at home. Just wondering how you are spending your Sundays back home. I guess the same old way.

So long for now. Not much more to say.

Love Joseph

* * * * *

THE DIARY OF JOSEPH DOGLIO

JUNE 26, 1943
DALHART, TEXAS

Hot today. Hot everyday. Hot, Hot, Hot.

* * * * *

JULY 6, 1943

Had my first guard duty today. They gave me a rifle with no shells. I guarded the mess hall. I did good. When my shift was over the mess hall was still there. It makes me laugh, I guess.

* * * * *

August 3, 1943

I don't drink coffee anymore. We get milk and more milk. No shortage of milk in the military. Maybe it's powdered milk. That's a hoot. A million cows in Texas and we get powdered milk. Oh, yeah, diary, we get bananas. Do we get bananas. Monkeys should be so lucky.

* * * * *

LETTER TO JOSEPH'S PARENTS

NO DATE

SANTA ANNA, CALIFORNIA

Hello Mom and Dad:

Just received your letter. Glad to hear you received the money. So you got it on Monday. Boy that letter sure made good time. Sure too bad about those boys drowning.

It won't be long until school is out. You'll have Junior home. So Johnny wrote home to say he is going to school. That is good. I had a letter from him about a week ago and he said all they do is drill, drill, drill.

Getting near the end of the page. Still the

same old life. I hope you had a nice "Mothers Day", Mom. I wish I could have been there. You were in my thoughts and most of all you were and always will be in my heart.

Love

Joseph

THE DIARY OF JOSEPH DOGLIO

MARCH 17, 1944
RAPID CITY, SOUTH DAKOTA

I find it difficult to explain my feelings. Today, March 17, 1944, marked my graduation from navigator school. I am now a Second Lieutenant in the Army Air Force. A Second Lieutenant. I feel so proud of what I have accomplished and yet what I am most proud of is that I feel so seasoned. I was like a boy, a country boy, and suddenly, almost over night, I have blossomed into an adult. Now I wait for the day to be tempered by fire; the fire of combat.

I wonder if my evolution is a result of the strict training or is it perhaps from the reality that my youth was somehow stolen from me by world events. My youth, what there was of it, consisted of innocent pranks played on youthful and inexperienced high school friends. My bashfulness, my shyness, and even my reserved mannerisms betrayed my desire to hold the hand of one of the pretty girls from my class. Someday, now that I feel older, maybe that will happen. I know not when.

This momentous war has consumed not only me, but it has consumed an entire world. I long to play my saxophone, play it for hours, for everyone to hear. Instead I move protractors, equate the reading of compasses and count the inches on rulers across my navigator's table. These simple tools are now my instruments. It is these simple instruments that make the music for our crew. One false note and we become lost in a sky that displays no helpful and beneficial road signs.

My exhilaration and joyousness is dampened by the absence of my family who understandably could not travel to Rapid City to witness the ceremony. I will share my joy by sending photographs of this august occasion.

Oh, by the way diary, I have no more boyish pimples. They are gone. My face is smooth as the skin of a ripened peach. Now that is really something.

MARCH 24, 1944
RAPID CITY, SOUTH DAKOTA

I was assigned a crew today. It was all very exciting. Lieutenant Hawkins is our pilot and Lieutenant Earl Hart is our co-pilot. I took a liking to Hart. He is low key, like me, and he appears to be meticulous in all he does. I noticed how he detailed our names on a piece of paper. He writes our names and then studies our faces with an intense glare. I found him studying me with his intense eyes. He seemed consumed with my appearance. Finally, he approached me.

He asked, "So you're the navigator?"

"I am," I replied.

"We'll see, Doglio. We'll see." He emphasized the 'dog' in Doglio. How do I tell him the 'g' is silent.

He made a good first impression, but with those matter of fact words I became aware that I had much to prove. My confidence in my ability to navigate a B-17 through the worst of weather had been bolstered by good marks in navigator school. Soon, I knew, I would be tested with my crew. God help me if I failed.

Lieutenant Cosco was our bombardier. The others were Bunning from Chicago, Garrett, O'Neill and a fellow named Schultz. I can't remember the name of our waist gunner but he seemed like a swell guy.

Lieutenant Hawkins informed us we would go through several practice runs. A short hop here and another short hop there. Then, on April 2, we are to fly cross-country to Boston, Massachusetts, our first taste, as a crew, of a long and tedious flight..

APRIL 2, 1944

We were awakened at 0400 hours. I managed a

quick breakfast of eggs and buttered toast. After checking weather conditions for our flight to the East coast, I discussed the route with Lieutenant's Hawkins and Hart.

I seem to detect an uneasiness about them. I get the impression they do not feel comfortable with me. I find it irritating. Maybe I am over reacting to my own apprehension. They don't know my ability to find a drop of water in the desert. I do and I have no reason to be concerned of my merits. I'm a shy country boy but I'll take care of my Fortress and her crew.

Of all the luck. The weather changed from calm winds and blue skies to a massive pattern of storms over the Eastern part of the United States. I instructed Lieutenant Hawkins to take us above the weather. We climbed to 26,000 feet, but not before a wild ride through storm tossed clouds. Hart asked several times if I had the altitude levels of the storm judged correctly. I assured him I did. When we broke through the "soup" he didn't acknowledge the correctness of my instructions. Just silence.

We flew above the weather for three hours and ten minutes. Our easterly course gave us a good tail wind. My calculations showed we were making good time. The cloud cover, heavy tail winds, and occasional cross winds were causing me to give constant updates to Lieutenant Hawkins.

Cosco, our bombardier, had drifted into a sleep

and upon awaking he asked, "You know where we are, kid?"

"Close to heaven," I replied.

"That's what I'm afraid of." His answer was sarcastic. It was not what I expected.

Lieutenant Hawkins, again on the interphone, asked for an update. The clouds below seemed to billow higher and higher into the sky. There was a low ceiling below us and we would not break through the cloud mass much before seeing the landing field.

"Sir," I told him, "you should begin your descent in exactly seventeen minutes." I gave him the rate of descent, the proper air speeds, and the timetable for landing.

"When you break through the clouds, Sir, the landing field will be directly in front of you, about 2000 feet below us."

I'm told Lieutenant Hawkins looked at Lieutenant Hart with a silent stare. Hart, I'm told, crossed his fingers.

Cosco spoke again. "I hope you got it right, kid. I hope you got it right.

I didn't reply.

The strong winds, severe lightning, and the purple darkness of the cloud cover gave our descent all the theatrics of a wild roller coaster ride. Cosco's face showed concern. He peered through the B-17 nose canopy searching for the ground.

His right hand played nervously with the bombsight.

"You should see the field in just about a minute, sir," I showered this knowledge on Lieutenant Hawkins. Cosco turned to stare at me, obviously not believing a word of my prediction.

Then, suddenly over the interphone, "Well I'll be damned. There it is." It was Lieutenant Hart. Cosco didn't look at me, he just reached back and touched my knee. His words were spoken with his hand. He squeezed my knee with all his strength. An acknowledgment of a sudden, and what would prove to be, an enduring trust. I could see his face reflected against the Plexiglass bubble. He was smiling from ear to ear.

The Fortress, being secured, we departed the plane. Lieutenant Hart approached me. "Doglio." He used the 'dog' again. "You are amazing. . ." he didn't finish his sentence. Everybody sort of jumped on me, smiling, hitting my back, and having fun. The tension was gone. We were, after one hair-raising flight, a crew. And a good one at that.

"Ah, Lieutenant Hart," I managed to summon him with my shy Midwestern constrained voice. "The name is Doglio. It's pronounced Do-leo. No 'g' sir. No 'g'."

"Well Dog," he smiled "you'll always be Dog to me. A bloodhound. You know. The kind of dog that can find anything," he paused and then added, "even in the worst weather."

I returned his smile. I nodded; thrilled we had this sudden belief in each other.

* * * * *

Later we learned we were being sent to England. Our departure date was May 2. Suddenly the reality hit me. The war was just an ocean away.

THE DIARY OF SECOND LIEUTENANT JOSEPH DOGLIO

MAY 1, 1944
AIR BASE, EAST COAST, USA

I had two dreams last night. The first was a terrifying scene of B-17's breaking up, wings falling from the fuselage. There were agonizing explosions that hurled both twisted metal and the burned human threads of once living bodies through the air in a frightening spasm of human conflict and death.

The second dream was a peaceful scene of angels and a sky full of spiritual peace. The faces of men, dressed in military uniforms, were a blur to me. Whoever they may have been there was no question of the peace and strength that accompanied their journey. Funny, but I could actually feel this strength. It was a power so great that I awoke with an indescribable sense of tranquility.

I sat on the edge of my bunk for what seemed an eternity.

Which dream was mine, I asked. Was it the first

or was it the second.

Then a strange thought entered my mind. What if both dreams belonged to me.

I fingered my Saint Christopher medal. Which dream was mine.

THE DIARY OF
SECOND LIEUTENANT JOSEPH DOGLIO

MAY 9, 1944
TROOP SHIP USS BRAZIL

I was thinking of home today. How I miss South Wilmington.

I remember the late fall evenings. Billy Finn and I would make our way to the edge of Joyce's bean field. We sat in the tall green and brown grass; we talked about everything. Girls, the return to school, the coal mines. We even talked about our favorite movies. I remember our conversations being both serious and amusing. Billy would laugh at a joke and I swear his laughter would carry across the Illinois prairie like some echoes from times past.

Every night, about 9:30, the heat lightning would illuminate the prairie sky. The bursts of electricity would begin in the west and slowly and silently they would come ever closer. Closer to where we sat.

The heat lightning was passive in nature. No bolts shooting from the sky. The lightning was not accompanied by claps of thunder. The friendly display of heavenly lights would stir our imaginations.

As the lights appeared overhead Billy and I would lay down, using the grass as a soft bed for our young bodies.

Then, looking toward the darkened sky, we would lay silently watching the beautiful show God had provided for us. Neither Billy or I spoke during this entire time. We left each other to his own thoughts and his own dreams. Sometimes I wondered what Billy was thinking and I know he often wondered what I was thinking. But we never asked. To break the silence would have been a disservice to the beautiful show of lights in the darkened sky.

As the heat lightning danced through the skies the music of nature would begin. First the cicadas started their steady drone. The prairie crickets, minutes later, would provide more harmony and at the proper time the tree frogs would add the bass for the unseen Illinois flat land orchestra. That's what Billy and I called them.

How I miss those peaceful times with Billy. We gazed at the heavens while Gods creatures provided the gentle music for our drifting minds.

Billy was always the first to break the silence.

"Play something." he would say in a hushed voice.

"What do you want to hear?" I answered knowing full well what his answer would be.

"Ave Maria, Joseph," he murmured "Play Ave Maria."

I would smile. My smile was not visible in the darkness as I reached for my saxophone.

"Okay Billy. Ave Maria it is."

The strains of the beautiful melody made their way across the bean fields and then, I know they did, they lifted to the sky above. The melody was always acknowledged by some unseen angel who on cue seemed to light up the darkened sky with a whole array of heat lightning that only minutes before was barely visible.

"They hear you," Billy nudged me. "I wonder why that always happens when you play that song?"

As the lightning filled the sky, I played as best I could. I was always moved by the response from the heavens.

Billy remarked, "Joseph, you don't suppose they really hear you, do you? Do you think the Holy Mother really hears the music and sees us laying here?"

I waited until I finished playing before answering, "Oh, I believe she hears us. Heck Billy, if she didn't, why would she react the way she does?" Then I pointed to the black sky above. "See, the lightning stopped. Just like it always does when I finish." I paused, "Oh, she hears us Billy. She hears us."

* * * * *

I haven't seen heat lightning since we left the States. I haven't played Ave Maria. I haven't seen Billy for a couple of years.

Someday Billy and I will be together again, standing side by side, reliving stories of our childhood. Keep Billy safe, Jesus. Keep him safe.

* * * * *

And so Billy did stand next to Joseph again. He did so on June 8, 1949. Billy Finn stood as a guard of honor beside Joseph's casket. One minute, while standing guard, someone noticed a tear appear under Billy's eye. Later the person asked Billy if he was okay.

He nodded his head and answered, "For a moment I remembered how Joseph would take his saxophone and play Ave Maria." Billy hesitated and then added, "No one played it better."

Just then Tillie Marketti joined the two of them. "It is only June and yet the sky is full of heat lightning. I can't believe how the sky is so alive with color."

Billy looked at her and then he walked to Joseph's casket. "Play it loud, Joseph. Play it loud so everyone can hear." Then Billy walked outside to look at the heavens. He was taken by the beautiful passive display before him. Then he was taken by the sound of cicadas, crickets, and tree frogs. The month of June was not the time for the Illinois prairie orchestra to play their nightly symphony.

He listened and watched for several minutes. Then he walked up the street and turned to make his way to the Saint Lawrence Catholic Church. Walking inside, he knelt before the Virgin Mother.

"You did hear him didn't you? You saw us laying in that grass."

The church was quiet. Billy didn't wait for an answer to his question. The answer, only minutes earlier, had been given to him.

THE DIARY OF
SECOND LIEUTENANT JOSEPH DOGLIO
JUNE 20, 1944
BASE 131, NUTHAMPSTEAD, ENGLAND

Scheduled for our first combat mission today. Target is Hamburg, Germany. Not a good first draw, but that's it.

The battle flags were flying over our Nissen Hut last night. I'm ashamed to say that I had the dry heaves all night long. I'm frightened of what we will face. I didn't think I would feel this way. I was sure I had prepared for this day, but obviously I have not.

Earl told me to drink lots of coffee. Don't know what coffee will do for me except make me want to, well you know, at 20,000 feet. I passed on the coffee. Let him try to take a leak while we are flying through German flak.

Flight time. Oh! yes. My first briefing was not what I expected. Really intense! Don't know what I expected, really.

JUNE 20, 1944

Where do I begin! My hands continue to tremble. Sorry! Can't write now.

* * * * *

Later. We are staying in the homes of newly acquired English friends. The sun has gone down and the warm beer, which I dislike, has a comforting effect on me.

We ran into heavy flak over Hamburg. We lost two engines and the *Angel* was shot up pretty badly. (Or is it bad?) Who cares! . Fire and black smoke billowed from one wing and then the other. *Angel* was being tossed about like a doll being shaken by some huge and unrestrained dog.

Dallas, after completing the bomb run, dropped from formation. We were sitting ducks for the ME's but they didn't come along. Dallas asked for a course home so I heeded the advise of other crews and took the *Angel* over the North Sea. We limped along on two engines. Losing altitude as we went. *Angel* continued to shake and shutter while dropping closer to the storm tossed waters below. Occasionally *Angel's* engines would cough and belch dark clouds of smoke into the unforgiving sky.

Dallas and Earl struggled with the controls. I

honestly don't know how they did it. Our fuel supply was getting low. Dallas and Earl thought of ditching in the sea. Our waist gunner lost control. He said, "No way!" His comment wasn't funny at the time but it is now.

I located an abandoned airstrip just a few miles from the English coast. We decided to give it a try.

Cosco nervously asked, "Where are we kid?"

I couldn't resist. I answered, "Close to heaven."

He threw his clipboard at me. We both laughed. How do you find room for laughter when you know the *Angel* might go down at any moment? We did. Broke the tension.

Dallas asked again. Are we on course, Dog. Damn, now he's calling me Dog.

"Sir, you bet your pilot's kazaza we are! You keep *Angel* in the air and I'll take you to the runway."

Cosco laughed again. "You got backbone kid, and you got guts."

I fingered my Saint Christopher medal. The token hung above my navigator's table. Saint Christopher protects me. Protects us all. It was all I could say. The medal danced to and fro, back and forth. Somehow I knew Saint Christopher would bring our group of weary travelers home.

We crossed the coast and sure enough, there it was. The sweetest looking abandoned airstrip in the world. Earl said the landing strip was too small to use; Dallas said we had no choice.

Needless to say, we made it. Barely. Dallas touched *Angel* down on the grassy field, our wingtips barely missing rocks on one side and huge trees on the other. When *Angel* stopped we were inches from a field of wheat. Garrett kissed the ground and Earl told Dallas he landed the *Angel* like a dog walking on one leg. Or something like that. I don't know.

Some English folks from the nearby village came by. We drank a pint or two and now we are finding some rest. I'm staying with a fellow named Granger. Seems as though he was a pilot during the first World War. He is an interesting character.

Before leaving *Angel* I noticed Dallas inspecting the fortress. He spent a long time looking at the painted face of our *Angel.* I didn't let on but I saw what he noticed.

I just returned from *Angel.* Sure enough there is a tear under her eye. It wasn't there when we took off, but so help me it's there now. How!! Where did it come from? Why is it there? It's spooky. I wonder if anyone else noticed the strange appearance of *Angel's* tear?

I'll worry about it tomorrow. Time for rest! I'm exhausted and thankful. Thank you Jesus for bringing us home. Thank you Saint Christopher for protecting us. You never fail me. And to you North Sea, I will forever challenge you to claim the life of a Doglio.

* * * * *

June 20, 1944, was the first combat mission for a B-17 Flying Fortress named *Angel*! Her crew, later known as the Angel crew, survived a perilous bombing run over the German city of Hamburg.

The B-17, *Angel*, lost two engines and suffered innumerable hits on her fuselage from the tiny steel shards of flak. Miraculously none of the crew was injured.

Second Lieutenant Joseph Doglio plotted a return course across the perilous North Sea. The flight over the cold, dark, treacherous waters was nerve racking. By "the grace of God" the *Angel* and her crew arrived safely in England.

Thus began the first mystery. Having inspected the fortress, Second Lieutenant Dallas Hawkins, *Angel's* pilot, discovered a tear had suddenly and mysteriously appeared under the *Angel's* right eye. Second Lieutenant Joseph Doglio, upon his inspection, also saw the tear. At first it was thought the tear was the residue from flak bursts that had hit the aircraft. This proved not to be the case.

Later, at Base 131, ground crew chief, Mark Dixon, tried to remove the tear. His attempts failed.

Sergeant Dixon later talked of the spirituality of the crew and the strange feelings he encountered while working on *Angel.* To this date there is no explanation for the tear, it's meaning, or how it suddenly and mysteriously appeared underneath the eye of the painted Angel. The tear on *Angels* face became a legend amongst the members of the Bomb Group.

The question most often asked is, "Did the tear symbolize the *Angels* fate?"

The answer is not found here. The answer lies in the continued mysteries of the Angel crew and their families. The answer is found in the events surrounding Anne Howard.

The real answer however, lies in a greater place. A place not of this world!

THE DIARY OF JOSEPH DOGLIO

JUNE 20, 1944
WAR RAVAGED SKIES OF EUROPE
THE FIRST MISSION

(This description of Joseph Doglios' first mission was found in his personal effects. It was not in his diary.)

Years of training never quite prepare a crew for the first combat mission. The real thing! Every new crew is baptized, not by fire, but by the words of crew members that have, after one mission, become veterans of the tumultuous skies of war torn Europe.

You learn of the times when entire squadrons became lost and somehow they suddenly appear in the midst of an entire formation.

Witnessing this event, we are told, is like being frozen in hell. That in itself is an interesting description of events. Frozen in hell. A pilot for a B-17 named *Beautiful Betty* told us that he has seen entire formations scattered and then, as they suddenly appear in the midst of a formation, a giant explosion erupts, as a B-17 rams into another and to his horror, he watched as the sky would become electrified in brilliant colors of reds and orange as exploding aircraft blew apart in what appeared to be a fleeting second of time.

The brilliant flash of the sudden explosion would sprinkle the heavens with burning debris: debris from aircraft and the debris of human remains as each piece of metal and burnt flesh slowly floated to the ground below.

Perhaps it's good to hear these stories. Maybe, in some small way, the stories prepare us for the possibility of disaster. In a way, we, all of us, are more careful, ever alert for the dangers of this unforgiving sky.

Now that we are finally airborne, Earl tells us to go on oxygen. I fasten my black oxygen mask to my face. I have done this many times before but today it somehow feels different. The mask seems to caress my face as though preparing me for the conflict that is to come. The rhythm of my breathing seems more pronounced. The accumulator, that moist and sticky bag, seems to talk to me in a unison beat of clicks and clacks.

We continue to climb. When will it end? When will we level off? Then, Lieutenant Hawkins, he just levels off and lo and behold we have made it through our first test. We are in formation, heading for the target.

I check my maps, then my watch. Looking at my

charts I know, that in a few moments, we will leave the English coast and soon we will be over occupied France.

Cosco poked my knee. He points through his bombardier Plexiglas. "Wow," I say aloud. All we can see is a sky full of B-17s. I, personally, had never before seen so many aircraft, all B-17 Flying Fortresses, filling the sky in what was an indescribable sight.

The flight was uneventful until Cosco once again touched my knee. Looking forward I saw a sky full of black, sooty, bursts of flak. The sky looked so ominous that I began to tremble. Within moments, the blue sky disappeared and the smell of powder and cordite filled the air. The sky no longer belonged to God; the sky belonged to the devil.

Then, in an instant, the lead B-17 piloted by John Godwin vanished in the burst of flak. Unmoved by it all, Dallas made a gentle and sweeping turn and we were on the bomb run. Cosco watched as we drew nearer to the black bursts of German flak.

The frightening sound of steel shards began to hit *Angel*. It sounded as though we were in a hailstorm but this storm was deadly. The flak was everywhere. Then an explosion, our number one engine was on fire. Oh God, not on our first mission!

"Mary Mother of God," I repeated this over and

over. . . "Mary Mother of God." My Saint Christopher medal swung back and forth in a wild and dizzy dance. It banged against the fuselage reminding me to keep faith in Saint Christopher's promise to protect me.

The sky turned completely black. We were in the midst of a flak barrage. Another engine is on fire. Dallas and Earl struggle to keep us in the air. *Angel* is struggling but somehow she holds on. She keeps flying. *Angel* must feel the pain but she ignores the agony and torment. She is on fire in two places and she is being torn and ripped apart by the devils instruments and yet this *Angel* strains to remain in the heavens. How does she do it?

I look at my watch. One minute to target. "Mary Mother of God," I say it again. I pray that the sooty puffs will not consume us.

I wipe my brow. Perspiration has gathered on my forehead. How can that be? It's twenty below up here. . . The heat from the devils fire has engulfed *Angel.* But I believe in the power greater that Satan. He will take us through this maelstrom. And Saint Christopher! He too will bring us home.

THE DIARY OF SECOND LIEUTENANT JOSEPH DOGLIO

JUNE 21, 1944
BASE 131, NUTHAMPSTEAD, ENGLAND

We had quite a discussion tonight. A member of the Chase crew said if there was a God, He wouldn't allow this war to happen. The conversation was taken up by everyone in the Nissen Hut. I just listened as the guys shared opinions on the subject. Carroll O'Neill didn't voice an opinion either. Like me, he listened attentively to what everyone had to say. His facial expressions gave me a clue as to what he was thinking.

Several fellows agreed with Lieutenant Smith, saying God must not care about the world if He allows such suffering and sadness. Others gave their opinion explaining why God truly exists and how He has a plan for the world.

Hearing enough, I grabbed my saxophone and walked outside. To my surprise Carroll followed me. We walked down the old Roman path until Carroll asked, "What do you think Joseph? You didn't say anything."

We stopped beside a hay wagon that was parked

next to a hardstand. “Well, Carroll,” I began. “I don’t think God created this mess. I think people created it. And I think the people who created it had help from a very powerful force.” I paused, “You know, Satan.”

“When it is over God will be sure it ends the way He wants it to. I think we are His army, and well, I don’t know Carroll. Sometimes I think we are like Michael, the Archangel. Don’t worry, He exists and He gives us the opportunity to live our lives. Sometimes we don’t do a very good job.” I looked at Carroll. “Do you see what I mean?”

Carroll fidgeted for several seconds, “Yeah, I think so. You mean He gives us rules but we don’t always live by them. Then we have to straighten out what we created.”

“Yeah. Something like that.”

Carroll shook his head and walked away. I wondered what was going through his mind. I wished someone like Father Sullivan or Reverend Duvall could have answered his question. I’m afraid I didn’t answer it very well.

“You going to play something?” Carroll called through the night.

“I think I will. What would you like to hear?”

There was a pause. Then Carroll reappeared through the night.

“Well, I think I would like to hear a religious

song. Do you know any?"

I smiled, "I know several."

"Then pick one. Just play something nice."

I thought for a few seconds and then I played a song my Aunt Jennie had asked me to learn.

I remember Carroll sitting on the path as the melody of the saxophone drifted across the base.

When I finished Carroll offered, "That was beautiful. What's the name of it?"

"It's called, 'How Great Thou Art'. "

"Do you know the words?"

"Yeah, I do. It was my aunt's favorite song."

Carroll pondered his response. "Joseph, tell me the words."

"Sure, Carroll." I placed my saxophone on the grass, "They go like this . . . ."

"Oh Lord, my God, when I in awesome wonder, consider all the worlds thy hands have made. . ."

THE JOURNAL OF ANNE HOWARD

JUNE 23, 1944
LONDON, ENGLAND

This day has been like a dream! I've kept pinching myself to see if I'd wake up! My day at the Admiralty passed as any another, but something quite unexpected happened while I was waiting for Margaret's shift, at the Red Cross Club, to finish. Throngs of Yanks with weekend passes were poring into Rainbow Corner in search of a room. The energy and volume were greater than usual, and so I found myself trying to be small to the side of the crowd. That's when I first noticed him. Joseph. He didn't see me looking at him right away, but before I could break my stare, our eyes locked. I'm not kidding; it was like something out of a fairy tale. I've never in all my nineteen years felt so utterly and completely exposed, nor at the same moment so comprehensive of the soul belonging to those eyes looking back at me. For me, the world stopped momentarily, like the way they say your heart stops beating when you sneeze. No sound, no motion. No Red Cross Club, only an all-encompassing certainty. That's when I became aware of the intensity and quickly shifted my attention to the floor . . .

As luck (or perhaps, fate!) would have it, this very same chap winds up in Margaret's line, and you won't believe this - she asks him and his friend Earl to join us for the evening!! Sly Margaret, winking at me as she handed him the keys to his room.

I couldn't believe that Margaret would be so bold as to ask two American soldiers to spend the evening with us, and a part of me worried that these two might have gotten the wrong impression. Father, after all, never tires of lecturing me about "brash American soldiers." But Margaret kept reassuring me that this Lieutenant, despite my worries, seemed especially nice, even a bit shy. So we waited for the two of them by the back window in the foyer, and all I can say is I was a bundle of nerves. What if he thinks I'm too young, or not sophisticated enough? What if he fancies Margaret? What if they don't even show up? Just as I was working myself into a tizzy, I saw the two of them walking toward us. Please be charming and worldly, I begged myself, feeling the blush rise in my cheeks. "Look sharp! They're here," said Margaret.

As the four of us shook hands, I couldn't help noticing a bashfulness about this Lieutenant Joseph Doglio, a self-consciousness that seemed somehow to mesh with my own sense of awkwardness. I also was instantly reminded of why my gaze had become fixed upon him earlier – quite handsome! Not wanting a repeat of the embarrassment I'd felt before when he caught me staring at him, I forced a quick, fluttery glance at his face as Margaret introduced us. "Anne volunteers at the Admiralty. That's why she wears that smart-looking uniform of hers," she was telling them.

Margaret and Earl kept a lively conversation going as we made plans for dinner. They talked with the ease of old friends. I was sorely aware of being the youngest in the bunch, keeping quiet for most of the walk to Dorchester Street, where Rolly had set aside a table for us at the Pub. Joseph also had said very little, and I wondered if perhaps he regretted his decision to join us . . .

For me, the evening finally took off when Rolly took over. It never ceases to amaze me. The way food can remedy the most awkward of situations. It was obvious these two hadn't enjoyed a good sit-down meal in some time, and both kept apologizing for their appetites. Rolly treated them as if they were his own, I must say, and even brought out his precious scotch in their honor.

But before he could pour a glass, Joseph leaned toward him and said softly, "Thank you, but Earl and I would rather you save that until you can celebrate your son's return from Australia." Rolly was visibly touched by this, and as he turned to leave our table, I could see his lips trembling as he fought back the tears.

Knowing how difficult things have been for Rolly since the war started, I felt tears welling up in my own eyes. I really didn't want to make a scene, so I was grateful when Joseph offered to walk outside with me for a bit of fresh air.

Because of the blackout, the streets were in total darkness; my little pocket torch was our only source of light as we slowly made our way down the street. Once I had gathered myself emotionally, I spoke. "I've known Rolly for years. He's the kindest soul you could ever hope to meet, never a harsh word for anyone. You know his son in Australia is about to go into combat, but what you don't know is that he's already lost one son in Africa. The death of her firstborn child really took its toll on Rolly's wife, and her health has been in a steady decline since. She has a heart condition, you see, and Rolly worries himself sick over her having another heart attack . . . "

That was when Joseph stopped and turned to face me. "Miss Howard, Ma'am, I hate seeing you get upset like this . . . " It wasn't his words so much as his gesture that caused the melting sensation I began feeling. "You have the face of an angel, Miss Howard," he said, softly thumbing the furrow out of my brow. "I'm sorry if I'm shifting gears abruptly, but I've wanted a few minutes alone with you all evening. It seems you and I met before we were actually introduced by your friend Margaret today, and I'm certain you know what I mean . . . " Somehow both of my hands were now resting in his as he continued. "Maybe it's all this talk of war and hardship that's giving me the courage to speak with you so directly, but I'm quite taken with you, Miss Howard. I realize I haven't had much to say this evening, but it's all been so overwhelming. London is huge. And you're so pretty . . .I haven't really known what to say. . ."

"Until now, I gather, Lieutenant," I said, confident the darkness was concealing my blush. "Well, seeing as we two are standing here holding hands, I insist that you stop calling me Miss Howard. It's Anne. And Joey – may I call you Joey?" Squeezing my hands slightly, he nodded his approval. "I've loved every moment of this evening, even the awkward ones," I said prompting a smile out of the both of us. "If anyone had told me this time yesterday that I'd be standing here where I now stand, having these feelings, I'd have thought them completely off their rocker," I continued. "Truths be known, I've never even been on a real date before, and if my father knew I was with you he would have a fit. He's a bit over protective."

"If he's over protective, it's because he cherishes you, and it's easy to see why," Joseph said. "I'll tell you honestly, Anne, I don't have a whole lot of dating experience myself. I've always been known to do my own thing; never had much time for it, I guess. Maybe I was waiting for the right girl to come along . . . "

I couldn't believe the things we were standing in the darkened street saying to one another! I've always considered myself on the shy side, and Mum and Da certainly haven't raised me to be familiar with blokes, but Joey isn't like anyone I've ever known. It felt perfectly natural for me to enquire as to his weekend plans, sensational, really! I asked him if he would allow me to show him around London tomorrow. I also asked him if he would accompany me to dinner and dancing at Covent Gardens in the evening. Yes, yes, he said yes!!!

He said he would love to! So, dear diary, it appears yours truly has her first official planned date tomorrow. Margaret is thrilled for me and is going to lend me the burgundy evening gown she knows I'm so fond of. I'm certain I can get reservations to Covent Gardens through the Admiralty. Oh, this truly has been the most incredible day of my life. I only wish that I didn't have to sneak behind my parents' backs to see him. .

THE DIARY OF SECOND LIEUTENANT JOSEPH DOGLIO

JUNE 23, 1944
LONDON, ENGLAND
RAINBOW CORNER RED CROSS CLUB

Sorry diary, don't know if I can write the perfect words to describe what happened to me today. You know, diary, I'm not much for the art of language but if I ever wanted to write something that was exact, exquisite, flawless, infallible, and pure, this would be the time.

I met a girl today. Her name is Anne Howard. I love her name. It's so gentle. Well, you know, it's soft, almost like a whisper.

Diary, she was not like other girls. There was something so fresh about her. She was refined and yet so shy. So neat and so virtuous.

I've searched for words but I can't find them; auburn hair, brown eyes, a face as soft and as pure as a newly fallen snow.

Anne was like a night full of stars. She seemed to

me to be like a place where the trees are all greener and a place where the sun is always brighter.

Do you know what I mean, diary? Do you know what I mean?

She's like a garden where there are flowers of all colors and yes, even like a place where there are no more bad dreams.

Anne gave me peace. Not only did she seem to be all those things but she made me feel that way; like gardens and flowers, and yes, like a bright shining sun. Is that the secret to love? Listen to me. I'm talking about love and I've only been with her for several hours.

God! I can't breath. I want to be with her.

THE JOURNAL OF ANNE HOWARD

24 JUNE 1944
MORNING
LONDON, ENGLAND

I could scarcely sleep a wink last night, and when I did sleep, I dreamt of Joseph. I dreamt the war was over, and we were walking through the most lovely rose garden. I remember thinking it odd that he was still in uniform, yet how dashing he did look! We were strolling, hand-in-hand, and the scent was so intoxicating. No words were spoken until Joey turned to me and said, "I will always be with you, sweet Anne." How cool and reassuring his hand felt as he softly stoked my cheek. . . Dreams can be so strange and beautiful. . .

Well, at any rate, I'm positively ecstatic about spending the entire day with my new American friend. I'm meeting him at 10:00 A.M. in front of the Pavilion. I hope he is as excited as I am! Mum and Da think that I'm volunteering at the Admiralty today, even though it is Saturday. I do feel terrible lying to them about this, but they would NEVER agree to let me run loose in London with a Yank! I am a grown woman, after all . . .

Well, I'm off, dear diary. I plan on having the most fabulous time of my life today. I'm leaving a little early, so as to make our dinner arrangements from a public telephone (can't be too careful!). I think I shall ring Captain McNulty at the Admiralty. I'm certain he can get us reservations at Covent Gardens. Oh, how full of surprises life can be!

* * * * *

24 JUNE 1944

EVENING

Dear Diary – It is 7:00 P.M. and I'm writing from Rainbow Corner. Margaret met me here with the burgundy dress at half-past. I'm to meet Joey downstairs in the foyer in thirty minutes. Oh, I'm so excited. I can hardly stand it! I feel I must write down everything that happens, everything I'm feeling, so that it can never be erased from my memory. After all, who would believe that on this very day I met the Prime Minister!? Joey and I met Winston Churchill this morning at Piccadilly! He just happened to be milling about at the exact spot where Joey and I had planned to meet. He was so gracious and friendly; I very near fainted when he asked my name. He asked me to "Be sure to show young Joseph here the best of our city." And, oh, how Joey handled himself! So courteous and handsome and smart. He said his heart was pounding in his chest, but he looked completely confident. I've never felt so proud in all my life! Mr. Churchill told him, "We appreciate each and every one of you Yanks." If only I could tell Mum and Da; if only they could have witnessed the Prime Minister shaking hands with Joey, then perhaps they wouldn't be so critical of Yanks. I hope one day I can tell them, and they will proudly realize that the efforts of brave young men like Joseph are what will ultimately bring this dreadful war to an end. I feel I'm the luckiest girl in the world to have met him! The rest of the afternoon we spent seeing the sights of the city. I took him to the tower of London, and we walked along the Thames. He wanted to see the changing of the guard and Big Ben, so we did that as well. I enjoyed seeing his reactions to these monuments I've grown so accustomed to, and felt at any moment I might abandon my sensibilities and throw my arms around his neck. I really don't know what's taken hold of me, but somehow it all seems natural, almost inevitable. The way we met, and how we savor every moment together, it all just feels right. I probably sound naive, considering we only just met, but who can I tell these things to, if not you, dear diary? I have to finish getting ready for our date now, but I'll be sure to tell you all about it later this evening. I can't believe I am finally going to Covent Garden! Anne Shelton is going to be performing with the Bert Ambrose Orchestra and everyone is trying to go. I do hope she sings "Berkeley Square" . . . Well, I'm off! Margaret is here to help me with the finishing touches...

* * * * *

24 JUNE 1944
LATE EVENING

Well, here it is eleven O'clock at night, and I've just finished lying to my parents for the second time about the most fabulous day of my entire life! The evening Joey and I shared at Covent Gardens was magnificent! I must say we made a fine looking couple. Walking down those stairs at Rainbow Corner, dressed in my beautiful borrowed gown and pearls, I felt like some Hollywood film star. Joey stood greeting me at the bottom of the stairs, his hat off, his eyes twinkling. "Anne, you look so beautiful," he said, taking my arm as I entered the foyer. It is a moment I will never forget.

We decided to walk to Covent Gardens rather than take a taxi, both of us wanting to make the most of our time together, alone. We turned many a head, the two of us locked arm in arm as we strolled the pavement. Joey looked especially fetching in his full dress uniform, so crisp and dapper! He spoke of his family along the way. They live in a small town called South Wilmington, Illinois, near Chicago. Compared to London it really is tiny, with a population of only 650! His parents are Kate and Albert Doglio, of Italian ancestry. I asked him what they would think about him spending his first weekend in London with a girl he barely knew? He said they'd be "the happiest parents in the world." I told him that I wished I could say the same – about my parents. I explained how infuriated my father would be if he knew I was being escorted to Covent Gardens by a Yank. This seemed to bother him, my having to make up stories in order to spend time with him, and well it should! I immediately felt sorry for even mentioning my parents, afraid I'd cast a pall on the evening's magic. I tried to change the subject back to his family and home, but he wasn't satisfied until I agreed to let him meet Mum and Da the next time he had leave. "I can't make any guarantees regarding my father," I confided, "But I'll bet Mum will end up being quite proud for me. I think she knows how I feel. I need someone to be close to . . ." I paused, then added, "I just never thought I'd meet someone like you. I'm so glad I met you, Joey." He turned to me and without saying a word, placed his hand softly on my cheek and kissed me. Me first real kiss!! I've always worried that I wouldn't know what to do when the time came, but it turns out my anxiety was for naught. It was the sweetest, softest sensation I've ever felt, and I prayed it never would end. We were standing right there in front of the entrance to Covent Gardens, oblivious to the scores of well-dressed, high-ranking people around us, when a voice startled us from our embrace. I suppose I feel more embarrassed for the public display now than I did at the time, brimming with emotion as I was. Joey and I were blocking the entrance, yet the couple that pointed this out to us couldn't have been nicer. They introduced themselves as Richard and Donelle Kirk, and we wound up sharing a toast of champagne (yes-champagne!) with them later in the evening.

Entering Covent Gardens was like stepping into another world – sheer paradise! If it hadn't been for all the uniformed attire, I could've easily forgotten there was a war going on around us. The main dining area was plush with all sorts of blooming plants, and the scent of the flowers created a gentle caress in the cool night air. The Bert Ambrose Band was fabulous! They were playing "I'll Get By," and Joey immediately asked me to dance. As we danced, I was suddenly reminded of my dream from last night, and a strong sense of deja vu swept over my body. Joey must have felt my shudder, as he asked me if I felt a chill. Without any forethought whatsoever, I heard myself blurting out, "Joseph, keep yourself safe. You will, won't you?"

I didn't want to tell him about my dream, about the lingering quality of it. I only wanted his words of reassurance, so that I might etch them upon my brain, to draw strength from when he was off fighting the war. I think he somehow sensed my need, pausing before he responded, as if searching for just the right words. Pulling me close, he whispered simply, "I will, Anne, I swear I will . . ." His breath was warm against my neck as we stood clinging to one another, not really dancing at all now.

We enjoyed an absolutely lovely candlelight dinner. Between the food, the wine, and the warm conversation, I began feeling a bit dreamy. The band kept at it, playing "The Nearness Of You" and "I'll Be Seeing You." Just as I was musing that this evening couldn't have been more magical, the bandleader Bert Ambrose announced Anne Shelton. I had been so enthralled all evening that I'd forgotten Anne Shelton was to sing! She opened with "A Nightingale Sang in Berkeley Square," and not a soul stirred. Everyone was riveted to the voice being projected off that stage. She's so young to have such a mature voice as that. When she sang a reprise of "Berkeley Square," Joey whisked me onto the dance floor. I knew it was to be our last dance of the evening, but for the curfew, I could've danced the night away.

I had to use the lavatory at Covent Gardens to

change back into my Admiralty uniform before I could come home. I felt like Cinderella! Joey and I both managed to find the reference humorous, laughing our way across the parking lot to hail a cab. That was when I heard a familiar voice call out my name from behind. "Miss Howard, is that you?" Instantly paranoid, I spun around to find Charles Spencer, date on his arm, grinning at me a few paces away. "Was it my imagination, or were you inside Covent Gardens tonight wearing a burgundy evening gown and pearls?"

Charles is an officer in the Royal Navy. We became acquainted at the Admiralty about a year ago. He's always been very kind to me, and I've sensed on more than one occasion that he admired me as more than an acquaintance.

After somewhat sheepishly confessing that, yes, that was me he had seen earlier inside, introductions were made. I hoped there would be no questions asked about why I no longer was wearing that beautiful gown and pearls, carrying them in a bag instead. To my relief, the conversation was brief and cordial. Yet I knew as we bid each other goodnight, the topic was bound to re-surface at some later date.

The cab ride home was all eyes and few words. The streets were in blackout, as usual, but tonight the darkness was our ally. There was plenty to say, but no need to say it. We just sat facing each other, hand-in-hand, smiling slightly, each preserving the texture of these final moments together. I suppose we both know the memory will prove invaluable as the war wages on . . .

I felt silly having to make the cab driver stop and let me out a full block from home, but I know Joey understood. Although fully aware he wouldn't be able to give me a precise answer, I had to ask when I would see him again. "As soon as I'm posted for leave, I promise you," his voice faltered slightly. With the cab meter running, we pledged to write to each other every day (Margaret's address will have to do for now). As I turned to leave, I heard, "Wait Anne, I just want to say that I . . ." When he didn't finish, I said, "I know, I know. I want to say it too . . . Thank you, Lieutenant Doglio." I leaned down and put my hand on his face, "Come back to me, Joseph." His skin felt cool, like it did in my dream.

THE DIARY OF SECOND LIEUTENANT JOSEPH DOGLIO

JUNE 24, 1944
LONDON, ENGLAND
UNDERGROUND SHELTER

As we left Covent Gardens the shrill sound of sirens signaled an air raid. This was my first experience of a German raid on London. We followed the crowd, hundreds of people, to the underground shelter. I was taken by the surroundings and how many people crowded into these make shift shelters. In some ways it was as though the people of London had made these underground tunnels their home.

The people of London sleep on makeshift beds. When they awake I wonder if they will be numbered among the homeless. Outside, in the city of London, bombs are falling everywhere. We can hear the faint explosions and the dull thud of the horrific concussions.

Outside this damp underground I know the searchlights are piercing the darkness searching for the German bombers. There will be fires and ambulances, heroics and agonizing death. More of London's streets will be left in rubble. Windows will disappear, water will be spouting from ruptured water mains and the hospitals will be taxed to the limit.

As I look around, these people, who somehow seem to endure this chaos, appear to take it in stride. Some fall asleep. I wonder if they have dreams and if so, of what? Do they dream of peace or do they dream of the horrors of war?

Whatever their dream, for the moment at least, they are in a safe place. The Civil Defense Wardens patrol the shelter, occasionally laughing with children who reluctantly return their smiles. I wonder if the children's smiles are genuine, or if they are a polite reaction to a man who gives them comfort and encouragement.

I begin to understand that these proud and courageous people have adjusted to this macabre dwelling.

The explosions diminish and suddenly they fade in the distance. We are told we can leave. Anne takes my hand. She smiles and nods. I believe she understands that this is my first experience in the underground. She doesn't say anything; she doesn't talk about it, she just moves forward, squeezing my hand as she goes.

We reach the surface. The air is thick with smoke. Fires can be seen lighting the sky. Some to the west, others to the north.

We walk quietly; we do not speak. Suddenly we are alone. The crowd has dispersed. Some returning to bombed out buildings that only hours before were homes that gave them peace and shelter. Others return to homes, untouched by German bombs, miraculously standing, and these people will give thanks for their blessings. Who decides what people will face tragedy and what people will give blessings?

"I think you may find this strange, Joseph. . ." Anne paused. "I have known you for forty-eight hours and yet I couldn't stand it if something happened to you." She held me again, tighter than before. "I don't believe I could go on. Oh Joseph! What have you done to me?"

I couldn't speak. I found no words. It was then I realized how vulnerable we were. Anne, here in London, defying air raid after air raid. Me in the sky over occupied France and Germany. Flak exploding all around me.

"Anne," I said, "I'm in love with you."

"I know Joseph. I know."

* * * * *

Now that I am alone a thought comes to my mind. When we bomb Germany do the people react in the same way as do the people in London? Are their spirits broken or are their spirits renewed? Are their spirits resolved to fight on?

THE DIARY OF
SECOND LIEUTENANT JOSEPH DOGLIO

JUNE 24, 1944 (PM)
LONDON, ENGLAND

Diary, yesterday was the most wonderful of days. I met Anne. But today was absolutely unbelievable. How can I be so fortunate? So blest as to meet such an incredible and extraordinary woman. She is nineteen. She works at the British Admiralty office. Anne is shy, like me, but we have begun to laugh and enjoy each other. She is beautiful beyond words. I believe Hollywood would say she is ravishing but to me she is delicate, charming, and even angelic. Her smile is gracious and genteel and I absolutely melt when she laughs at the most insignificant things. I swear I have fallen in love with her. Can that be possible?

Today, while walking from Rainbow Corner, we saw a large crowd gathering on the street. We explored and found none other than the Prime Minister, Winston Churchill, talking with the crowd as if he were merely a passer by. Anne, losing her shyness, pushed through the crowd until lo and behold we were standing directly in front of him—Churchill.

Anne, in her uniform, and me, in mine, drew his attention and he spoke to us. Not a living person in little old South Wilmington will believe this. He shook my hand and he instructed Anne to give me a tour of London that I would always remember. Astonishing stroke of luck but it was Anne who made it happen. Uniform or no uniform, if I were the Prime Minister, I would have spoken to her too.

As the day went on we became so taken with each other. I could feel Anne's tenderness and her concern for me. Genuine concern. She is swell. I hope I have made an impression on her. I want to because even now my heart feels so empty without her.

Tonight we are going dancing and we will have dinner at Covent Gardens. Anne said it is an elegant place. Anne Sheldon is supposed to sing. Anne said she (Sheldon) is only thirteen years old with the voice of an angel. How exciting to have this time together.

Oh, we had several hilarious moments today. Seems we speak the English language but our words sometimes have different meanings. Anne laughs at me and at the way we

Americans speak. She says we have absolutely undone the art of language. She is kidding of course but it is funny.

Anne, during our talks, said her father was in desperate need of bags. I found that to be peculiar but then again, I thought, maybe he needs bags in his home or at his work. I told Anne I could get bags from our cook at the base.

Confused, she asked why a cook at the air base would have bags to give away.

Well, one thing led to another, and we found ourselves in front of the Red Cross Club. Telling Anne to wait I ran inside and asked the volunteer if she had a few bags to spare. As luck would have it she suddenly produced eight paper bags. I was so excited I almost ran into a Major who was standing near the door. I ran into the street, held the bags behind my back, and then surprised Anne by showing her the bags and saying – "For your father." I was so proud.

Anne began to laugh. A chuckle at first. Then a hilarious roar until tears rolled down her cheeks.

Somewhat embarrassed I stood there, seemingly naked, as people stared at the two of us. Heaven knows my face turned red as a beet. Anne laughed. She threw her arms around me and said, "Oh, Joseph, I love you." That was it; I'll never be the same. When she said it, her words just seemed to go straight to my heart. I'll marry Anne someday. I know I will.

Anne took the brown bags and walked down the street. She would take four or five steps, stop and laugh, and then look at me and say, "Oh, Joseph, you are so precious." Then she would walk some more, laugh and say we Yanks were all a loveable bunch of cowboys. Especially me.

Finally, after several minutes of Anne carrying on I asked her why all of this was so funny? Again she held me and this time she repeated what she said earlier. We Yanks had absolutely demolished the English language. She proceeded to tell me that bags, in the proper English language, meant trousers, not brown bags as I had given her.

Then I laughed, we both laughed. We held each other. It was, this moment, the greatest feeling of my life. If feelings could talk this pleasure would be described as a symphony of sound played to perfection.

Then we became a little giddy. I went into a shop, found a pair of scissors and cut two holes in the bottom of one of the bags. Returning the bag to Anne, I said, "Here you are. Now maybe this bag will fit your father." With that we sat on the curb and laughed until our stomachs hurt. In a million years I wouldn't have done that. Anne sets me free. I'm alive when we are together.

I must go diary. She will be here soon. Dinner and dancing. I've not done this before. I wonder if Anne has? Should I ask? No, I think not. It doesn't matter.

Oh Anne, if I could only find the words to tell you how I feel.

THE JOURNAL OF ANNE HOWARD

25 JUNE 1944
LONDON, ENGLAND

When I woke up this morning, I felt like cursing the war. But it is precisely due to the war that Joseph and I were allowed to meet. I pray and pray for this dreary war to end, but it has brought me a romance I never dreamed possible. I knew the instant I saw him at Rainbow Corner that something clicked inside of me, that I had suddenly been drawn into a situation over which I had little or no control. I've never felt so blissful in all my life, nor so apprehensive. If only there were some way I could protect him, shield him from the imminent dangers of war. All I can do is pray. I love you, Joseph Doglio! How it is possible for me to feel this way so suddenly, so unexpectedly, I do not know. I wanted to tell him last night how I feel, but it just seemed too much. Though looking back over the time we shared the last two days, I believe I have conveyed my love for him. Subtlety can have a very lasting impression, after all . . . Oh, please God, please keep Joseph safe. Keep his entire crew safe.

I'll work even harder at the Admiralty, I'll help out more at home. I will do whatever you need me to do, God, to bring this war to an end, finally. And I vow the next time I see Joey, I will tell him how much I love him, even if he doesn't feel the same way for me. And I hope I can see him soon, or else I'm certain my heart will burst wide open!

THE DIARY OF
SECOND LIEUTENANT JOSEPH DOGLIO

JUNE 26, 1944
NUTHAMPSTEAD, ENGLAND
BASE 131

Captain Ross, our Flight Commander, and Major Rooney, our Squadron Commander, led the mission today. We hit Bachmont, France. There were twelve crews from the 602nd today. All together the 398th put up fifty-two crews to hit the target. We plastered it, too. Direct hits by all groups.

So far it's been, Hamburg, Germany, Rouen, France, and now Bachmont. Twenty-two more.

JUNE 26, 1944

Man, the battle flag is up over our Nissen Hut again. Another mission tomorrow. That's three out of the last four days. I wonder where we will go tomorrow.

The flak gets on our nerves. Tomorrow will be our fourth mission but already I can see the strain in the faces of some of the guys. We seem to grow old fast here. No time to play jokes or even laugh. I don't remember the last time we goofed around. I think it was when we landed safely after the Hamburg mission. No time to laugh I guess. Fly, debriefing, sleep, wake up, briefing, and fly. All the time hoping that a piece of flak doesn't have your name written on it. Even Earl appears more somber. They have to give us a break soon; but then again with the Infantry trying to bust through the German defenses I guess we will have our share of flying. D-Day was successful and now it's on to Germany. I feel sorry for the foot soldier. I can't even comprehend what he must be going through.

JUNE 27, 1944

We went to Toulouse, France today. Thank God, it wasn't a bad mission. Little flak and not one German fighter. Saint Christopher continues to protect us.

Cosco was hamming it up a little. Good to see him laugh. He made me laugh a little. Hawkins said he was going to separate the Italian guys. We might start a mutiny and take the *Angel* to Rome. That's a hot one. I said that's a hot one.

* * * * *

JUNE 28, 1944

Oh sweet Jesus! Thank you! No mission today. Wrote a letter to Anne, mom and dad. I even sent a letter to Junior and Aunt Pauline. Writing a letter gave me some time to relax.

Anne is on my mind. Diary, I can't tell you how much I want to see her. I think of her every waking moment. Can I ever tell you how beautiful she is.

Earl and I played a little baseball today. I did something I haven't done in a long time. After playing ball, at dusk, I pulled out the saxophone. The guys were surprised that I could play so well. Garrett asked me to play *Danny Boy* and Earl asked me to play *Amazing Grace.* Before I knew it I had a crowd of guys around me. Even Sergeant Dixon came by. It was a swell time for all of us. Funny what a little music will do for our spirits. Oh by the way. I really like Sergeant Dixon.

Oh no! Battle flags again. Not again! We go up tomorrow. Oh sweet Jesus! Be with us.

* * * * *

JUNE 28, 1944
EVENING

One of the guys from another crew went a little crazy tonight. I heard he completed his eighteenth mission today. After debriefing he just lost it. When things like that happen we feel a little down. We shake it off though. Funny how we small town boys, fellows from the city, and even guys who live on farms adjust to this kind of life.

Just several weeks ago we trained for war but really knew nothing about war, except what we saw in the newsreels.

Then one day we are flying our *Angel* to a target, releasing our bombs, killing people, and then we fly home. If we are lucky our enemy won't be successful in killing us.

Strangely enough none of us wants to do this but we haven't been given much of a choice. Adolph and the Japs started this whole mess and we can't allow them to finish it. We'll do that and boy when we do I know this will be the last war. After all, who in their right mind would want this type of human misery to happen again? Uh ah-no more wars. Not after this one.

Earl just threw his pillow at me. "Go to sleep," he yelled. I smiled at him and shut off my penlight. Somebody farted. Smells so bad. Earl told everybody not to light a match.

THE DIARY OF SECOND LIEUTENANT JOSEPH DOGLIO

JUNE 29, 1944
NUTHAMPSTEAD, ENGLAND
BASE 131

Evening. Mission to Biennais, France. Turner led the mission. The 398th caught living hell today. It all began during take off. The first B-17 to take off lost power and clipped the trees at the end of the runway. We later learned everyone survived but the 17 was pretty banged up.

Second, we ran into a hornet's nest of ME's. They did their best to break our formation but thanks to our pilots the integrity of the formation held fast.

One ME was hit by one of our guys. Looked like it blew apart but I couldn't tell exactly. It seemed to drop uncontrollably through our formation and miraculously didn't hit any of us. That was lucky, I think.

Thirty minutes before beginning the bomb run another group of ME's took a swipe at us. *Angel* was hit several times, one cannon shell coming through the nose section, just missing me and John.

Then we wheeled into the bomb run. The ME's broke away and we headed straight into a heavy barrage of flak. What was so unusual about the flak was that it was so accurate today. These guys manning the 88's down there were pretty darn good.

Then all hell broke loose. The devil was at work in the sky as well as on the land. Flannigan, on our wing took a hit in the tail section. He tried to hold his position but it was impossible. Fire erupted from one engine and the Fortress just started down, spinning as it went.

John was yelling, "Get out, get out!" but I don't think anyone made it. We didn't see any chutes.

Then Milliken got hit. They burst into flames and the guys started bailing out. Don't know how many.

While all this was going on Dallas plodded along towards the target. The flak was bursting all around us. The shards of steel were flying everywhere. We could hear them bouncing off *Angels* skin. "Hold together *Angel*," I said. Saint Christopher was once again banging against the navigator table and the fuselage.

Two more Fortresses took hits. One was Kiner, the other Jameson. Jameson's plane was named *Too Tough*. I hoped the name was fitting. Maybe they would make it.

Kiner fell from formation. They didn't make it. I understand the crew bailed out. *Too Tough* made it home. I don't know how but she did. The rudder was almost blasted away and the left wing had a giant hole through it. Part of the fuselage on the co-pilots side was just hanging there. It must have been flapping in the wind during the entire flight home.

John finally uttered those words I listen for, "Bombs away, Skipper." Then we were on our way home. About fifteen minutes into the return leg home our little friends joined us. They are a welcome sight on this day.

The wind whistled through our positions thanks to the hole in our fuselage. Cold as can be. My teeth are chattering but at least I can feel the cold. Some of our guys won't feel anything anymore.

* * * * *

We are always a little scared. I am, but now it's becomes a job. Almost a daily routine. We seem to be in the air constantly. No time to be afraid anymore. Just do our jobs is about it. I wonder if the fear leaves us or if we just become accustomed to it? (Fear) Maybe that's how life is. We adjust to what the events give us and that which was once unheard of is now an everyday occurrence. None of us enjoy this but we do it. Tension is always there but we are veterans now. What bothered us earlier is just part of our life now. I long for peace. Peace was so good.

THE DIARY OF
SECOND LIEUTENANT JOSEPH DOGLIO

JUNE 30, 1944
NUTHAMPSTEAD, ENGLAND
BASE 131

I miss her so much that I can't describe my feelings. I can't sleep; my back feels like a giant weight has been placed between my shoulder. I take deep breaths because my lungs labor for air. I wonder if this is my first encounter with love or is it a passing infatuation. Is this some kind of foolish obsession or even madness that has engulfed and consumed my heart and mind? What's happened to me?

Earl has noticed my personality change. He teases, good naturedly, about my sudden mood change. He says I'm in love like a coon hunter who has a passion for good dogs. Gees, I told him, can't you come up with something better than that. Bunning barks every time he sees me. I'm doomed. Hart has done it to me again. Somehow he always likens me to a dog.

The only time I function like a normal human being is when we are flying. I was good, but now I'm better. It's not the crew that brings out the best of my skills. It's my desire to return home to Anne. What I wouldn't give for a three-day leave.

I wonder how she is. What she is doing. I wait to see her. What will mom say when I tell her?

THE DIARY OF SECOND LIEUTENANT JOSEPH DOGLIO

JULY 1, 1944
NUTHAMPSTEAD, ENGLAND

I've really not written about our crew. The crew of *Angel*! I guess I have mentioned them from time to time, but only in passing.

Well diary, we are a good crew. A religious bunch of guys; from my Saint Christopher medal to little spiritual verses the fellows have taped next to their stations. We all have a common God. A common belief, too!

Only O'Neill, our tail gunner, seems unsure of religion. But even he has begun asking questions and he has now hung a photo of blue sky next to his tail gun position. He has a note above simply saying, "I'm trying." I think he means he is trying to understand our religious beliefs. Well, I think that's what it means.

We work well together. I know we worry about each other but that's good. It means we care. I especially like our co-pilot, Earl Hart. We talk a lot. He talks of his home in Marion, Virginia. Seems like he enjoys hiking through the mountains near his home. He seems to like the outdoors. We made a promise that when this war is over we will go on a fishing trip together. Me and him and a bunch of worms.

He has a girl friend back home. Her name is Alpha. Talks about her all the time; she must be special.

Earl likes to be an actor, too. A real actor! He tells me he used to act in college. That's hard for me to believe but he swears by it. He told me the story of how he couldn't remember some lines in one of his plays. He claims he was so mad, during practices, that when the play was over, he took his play book and put it away where not a soul could find it. Says he will go home someday, give it to his mom for a remembrance of his frustration, but more for the way she used to imitate him when he couldn't remember the lines. Earl said his mom would get a real kick out of seeing the book again.

Well, I'm tired diary. More about the crew later!

* * * * *

Second Lieutenant Earl Hart, from Marion, Virginia, didn't make it home. He did not have the opportunity to share the memory of his play book with his mother. It was something he dreamed of doing because, he said, it would make mom happy.

On August 12, 1948, four years after his death in *Angel*, Vena Hart, Lieutenant Hart's mother, was moving to a new home. The old home held too many painful memories. During the move, Vena Hart noticed a worn, discolored book turned upside down on the family piano.

She didn't recognize the book from a distance. She walked to the piano to take a closer look. There, on the piano, was Earl's play book. The page number exposed was page twenty-one. The words were underlined with a note in Earl's handwriting. "Why can't I remember these lines?"

Vena Hart began to cry. Her husband, Ambrose, entered the room and asked, "What is it Vena? What's wrong?"

Her answer was, "He's come home Ambrose. Our son has come home."

THE MYSTERIES
A MIRROR TO THE PAST

PRESENT DAY 2001
CHAPEL HILL, NORTH CAROLINA

The accounts of the *Angel* mysteries were detailed in the book, *Angel: A Mighty Fortress.* The stories captured my imagination and now, several years later, the mysteries of the B-17 Flying fortress and her crew continue to intrigue me. The strange and spiritual circumstances surrounding the families of crew members, and, yes, Anne Howard have at times consumed my every thought. What is more fascinating to me is the brief description of these mysteries as found in the journal of Anne Howard. Her words reflect an acceptance of all that happened. Her faith and confident convictions in miracles are highlighted by her devotion to her trust in God.

This is what she wrote. . . .

THE JOURNAL OF ANNE HOWARD

27 JUNE 1944

THE TEARDROP

Joseph told me about *Angel's* teardrop. How it mysteriously appeared under her eye. I have given thought to the meaning of it all. On one hand I fear it is a terrible premonition of things to come. On the other, I trust that if it is a bad omen then surely God must think well enough of this crew to prepare them for what is to come. The image that I prefer to believe is that God has chosen this particular *Angel*, painted by a human hand, to cry for a troubled world. Either way, whatever may be the case, I honestly believe there is a spiritual reason for this amazing riddle.

FEBRUARY 1969
THE PASSAGES

A reunion with Sergeant Mark Dixon. How lovely to see him again. He is a gracious man. He continues to cherish Joseph and the crew of *Angel*. I believe with all my heart that he is a religious person. I find it difficult to describe him. He has this spiritual presence about him. He seems to radiate a certain honor, or perhaps it is duty. Whatever it may be, his actions serve him well. I like Sergeant Dixon. I'm happy he returned to England for the 398th reunion. I'm thankful for the time he spent with me. *(Then Anne Howard wrote about various events that took place during the reunion. She then returns to a discussion she had with Sergeant Dixon.)*

The good Sergeant, with his delightful southern accent, told me about the verses he found at the crew members stations (on the B-17 named *Angel*).

I am stunned to learn that the message found at Joseph's navigators table read. . .

Comfort one another, for my God and a host of angels will comfort me.

Did Joseph know his fate or did some spiritual force cause him to give thought to his future.

Second Lieutenant Earl Hart had written. . .

Weeping may last for the night but a shout of joy comes in the morning. An angel will comfort you and her tears will be no more.

I fail to grasp the meaning of what dear Earl may have been thinking but could it be he too was guided by some uncanny knowledge of what was to come.

Even more puzzling are the words of pilot, Second Lieutenant Dallas Hawkins. . .

Through my fortress I will find peace and eternal life.

I must have looked so startled as I remarked to Sergeant Dixon, "They knew, didn't they? They all knew their fate."

Poor Sergeant shook his head and then I said it again, "They knew!"

The bombardier had written. . . *Be true to your friends for they shall wait for you always.*

I'm told the bombardier, who did not fly on the day of *Angel's* final mission, is still alive. His message is so appropriate isn't it. His friends wait in a higher place while his loyalty remains true and strong.

The waist gunner and the tail gunner had written messages as well. Having listened to Sergeant Dixon's recollection of their words I have no doubt in my mind that angels were indeed a presence in the lives of the crew.

Now after all these years I understand my feelings. Somewhere Joseph is near. My imagination of his closeness is not imagination at all. He is my constant companion. The man I love has always been with me. He never left my side.

* * * * *

Sergeant Dixon told me about the play book that suddenly appeared in the home of Earl Hart's parents. A play book lost for years and a play book that gave hope to a mourning mother.

There was the marvelous story of Joseph's bedroom window. How it was mysteriously opened on the day of Joseph's funeral.

Oh sweet Joseph how you enjoyed the fresh air of your prairie town.

My excitement reached such a level that I seemed to startle dear Sergeant. "It was Joseph. He came home to his mother."

Then to Sergeant Dixon, I told the story of the locket's return. His only response was, "I'm not surprised."

I enjoyed our time together. Sergeant Dixon and me. He is the most genteel man. We made a promise to see each other again. To stay in touch. We said a prayer together. It wasn't a prayer, really. He just took my hand, bowed his head and in his slow, and deliberate way said, "Keep them close, Father. Keep them close."

I found a tear falling from my eye. I seemed to tremble for a moment. The picture of a B-17 and a crying angel entered my mind. I allowed my tear to make its way down my face and then, squeezing Sergeant Dixon's hand, I said, "Yes, please keep them close."

I accompanied him to the airport. We said our goodbyes. He showed me a photograph of his wife. She was a beautiful lady. Short with a touch of blonde hair. She had a smile that radiated kindness.

"She's not well," he said as he returned the photo to his wallet.

Then, with some reservation, I removed a photo of my dear son, Joseph, from my bag. I handed it to him, "My son. He is a pilot in the Royal Air Force." It was all I said.

This wonderful man studied the photograph and then smiled. "Joseph would have loved him." His smile turned to understanding. He looked me directly in the eyes and I seemed to waver. Then he embraced me and said, "God Bless You. Both of you." And he was gone.

As he disappeared in the crowd I asked the question of myself, "How does he know? How could he have known the truth?"

* * * * *

THE THOUGHTS OF AUTHOR DON GADDO

There were other mysteries of course. The dream of a nurse, the encounter I had with an angel, the unexplained and miraculous recovery of a Jaguar fighter bomber as it sped toward the North Sea in a spiral of death and, of course, the miraculous recovery of Connor Dahm, a child with an irreparable heart condition. There was the Sunday morning in 1998 when James Kiernan saw eight men, dressed in World War II uniforms. Their mysterious appearance on an island near Cashiers, North Carolina remains the deepest mystery of all.

And there is the story of the day in South Carolina when Sergeant Dixon rejoined his cherished crew. The story of that triumphant day is told in this book.

* * * * *

I refer to these stories as mysteries. That's what people prefer to call them. But in the deepest depths of my heart I consider these stories to be miracles. The miracles of a world that sometimes hides all that is good and yet allows us to seek His message of what awaits us in some mysterious place that lies far beyond our imagination.

Albert Einstein once said *The most beautiful thing we can experience is the mysterious.*

And so it will be. . . .

THE DIARY OF
SECOND LIEUTENANT JOSEPH DOGLIO

JULY 4, 1944
NUTHAMPSTEAD, ENGLAND
BASE 131

Big celebration today! Big band and fireworks! It was swell. I noticed Garrett and Schultz dancing with every girl that was bussed in by the Red Cross. Garrett is only nineteen but boy he can dance. I'd pit him against any fancy dancer in the US. His feet are as happy as a lark. They never quit moving. I swear he could light a fire under the soles of his shoes.

Shucks, he's better than anyone on the base.

THE JOURNAL OF ANNE HOWARD

2 JULY 1944
LONDON, ENGLAND

It has been a week and still I've received no word from Joseph. I've been keeping as busy as possible, as work keeps my tendency to worry and fret at a manageable level. Still I'm constantly imagining what new horrors Joey is finding himself faced with from day to day. I try picturing my love for him as a protective aura, a shield that visibly surrounds him, but in my heart I know this bloody war isn't selective in choosing its victims. I continue to pray. What else can I do?

Mum reads me like a book. I've tried denying that anything is the matter, but she sees right through my charade. I think she's known right from the beginning that I've met someone, and that furthermore that someone happens to be a Yank. She's been very gentle in her inquires, I must say. I've tried explaining that my moodiness of late is directly linked to the increasingly frequent air raids we've been experiencing.
I also tried blaming work: all the horrifying war stories I hear

about at the Admiralty. Basically I just attribute my mood swings to the war, war, and war! She hasn't tried to delve any deeper, but I can see the concern in her face. I know she wants what's best for me, and I'm actually yearning to tell her the whole truth. I think if I could be completely candid with Mum, I'd feel much less tense about everything. In fact, the more I consider it, the more I'm encouraged to have a heart-to-heart with her this very evening. Yes, that's what I'll do!

THE JOURNAL OF ANNE HOWARD

5 JULY 1944
LONDON, ENGLAND

Where are you, Lieutenant Joseph Doglio? Why haven't I heard from you? I tell myself that if something dreadful has happened to you, I would sense it somehow, but the truth is I'm terrified for your safety.

Please come back to me, Joey.

Please let my love be a beacon in this time of darkness and despair.

Please being this war to an end, God.

Please. . . .

THE DIARY OF SECOND LIEUTENANT JOSEPH DOGLIO

JULY 6, 1944
NUTHAMPSTEAD, ENGLAND
BASE 131

A clear morning! You can actually see the stars. The sky if full of them. We've had more than our share of rain. I remember sitting in my yard, at home, looking into the black skies of the Illinois prairie. There were times when it seemed that there were so many stars that a person could jump from star to star without ever missing one of those sparkling and twinkling lights from heaven.

There were times when I looked in wonder. As a star fell from the darkened mid-western sky, I often wondered why it fell or what made it fall. I watched the fiery light shoot through the sky at great speeds, and then suddenly it would burn away, extinguish itself never to be seen again.

That's how life is here, at Base 131. We are so young. We are so many youthful shining lights and one day several of us are gone. Our youthful and vigorous lights falling from the sky, brightly lit in brilliant orange fireballs, until suddenly, like a falling star, the light of young men are extinguished forever.

Then I ask the same questions; why did it happen? Why was that Fortress and crew chosen to fall from the sky? Lights forever extinguished, never to be seen again. What remains perhaps is a faded memory of someone who only hours before brightened your day, like a star, with a warm smile and cheerful "good morning."

Star light, star bright,
First star I see tonight.
I wish I may, I wish I might,
Have the wish I wish tonight.

I wish that this agonizing and horrible war would end tomorrow.

* * * * *

JULY 7

I knew yesterday was too good to be true.

Briefing just finished. Sweet Jesus, we are going to Leipzig, Germany today. This will be a tough one. I feel it in my bones. Colonel Hunter provided the briefing. He is really a good guy. At least I think so.

The crews, all of them, seem a little tired today. Maybe it's because it's Germany. We always catch the devils fury when we go to Germany.

Later. Returned safely from mission. Just finished debriefing. We plastered the target. Bulls' eye on all counts. No losses but several Fortresses were shot up pretty bad. *Horse Sense* had several chunks out of its wing and fuselage. The turret gunner was hit but we hear he's going to be okay. Several other fellows were wounded today. Thank goodness no serious injuries.

We are thanking our lucky stars that a mission to Germany was carried out without a single loss.

* * * * *

EVENING OF JULY 7

It can't be! The battle flags are flying again. Three days in a row. I wonder where we will drop our bombs tomorrow? I wonder if we will be as fortunate as we were today?

Wrote a short note to Anne. I long for a few days with her. Just an hour would do.

* * * * *

JULY 8, 1944

The target will be Humieres, France. I hope it's as easy as Cauchie-D' Ecques. Father Sullivan was giving his blessings. So was the good pastor, Reverend Duvall. I think Duvall is a grand fellow. He's so easy to talk too. Catholic, protestant, or even a Jewish prayer. Religion is not different anymore. One God, one prayer, one blessing, and if it is His will, one death (or more - or none). Funny about religion. So many differences and yet here in the middle of war, there are no differences. Suddenly we are all asking the same God for His tender mercy. When the war is over we will likely disagree on this and that all over again. In these days of anticipation there is no this and no that, just Him. So strange at times.

Angel, as usual, is glowing its usual vivid morning color. The sun casts an eerie glow over her aluminum fuselage. As I look around I can honestly say *Angel* always seems brighter than the other B-17's. I wonder why that is?

Really, I mean it. *Angel* just glows, almost spiritually. The tear under *Angels* eye has made our crew the topic of conversation around here. Everyone speculates about the meaning of the tear. We are asked about it quite often. I find it difficult to answer the questions because I think there is a reason for this mystery. I don't want to admit what I think about it. Sometimes it's unsettling and other times I look at it as a gift from God. Sort of like He is asking us a question-"Do you believe?" You know what I mean.

Angel captivates Dixon. He constantly talks to Dallas about her. We keep no secrets from each other. We all discuss *Angels* tear. Dixon tried to remove it but he admits it will not budge. He is religious, like us, and he treats our Fortress as though it is a real angel. He says God has a hand in all of this. We'll see - We'll see. I quietly wonder what our Lord has in store for us?

* * * * *

We are in a state of shock. It was much too close today. My thoughts are so tangled that I can't write. I'll wait until later. Maybe much later. We were close to being a falling star today. Very close! I even prayed the rosary while holding John and Saint Christopher.

* * * * *

Humieres, France. The ME broke through the entire formation. He was alone. A bloodsucker as we call a lone German fighter. Every weapon from every Fortress took aim at him. We all missed, but he didn't.

He hit *Angel* with everything he had. The entire bombardier Plexiglàs shattered and fell away. I ducked and covered my face, little good it did. When I opened my eyes I was covered in blood. I felt no pain. Then I realized it was John (Cosco) that was hit. He was hit bad. The wind was blowing through the nose section. The whole section was gone. All of it. Blown away by the ME's cannon. Before I could grab John, I thought we would both be sucked from the plane. *Angel* started to dive. The dive prevented us from moving. The force of our free fall held us against the fuselage. It looked like it was all over.

Then, as if by some miracle, *Angel* slowly began to right herself. We were out of formation but we appeared to be okay. The wind was blowing through the bombardier opening, unobstructed, and the temperature just seemed to drop to 100 degrees below zero.

Earl said Dallas was hit, but he (Earl) had control of *Angel*. Cosco was bad. Really bad. He was bleeding from several wounds. His eyes seemed to beg me to do something. Somehow I managed to patch him up. I gave him morphine and held him as best I could. The *Angel* was full of holes. I honestly thought we would bail out. I don't know how Earl brought her home.

I noticed a large hole above the navigator's table. How did the shell miss me? It's placed at head level. Exactly where I was sitting. Saint Christopher, despite the turbulence from the wind, just moved slowly, back and forth. I managed to take the medal in my hand. It felt warm. I'm sure it can't be. If it wasn't, how can I feel the heat through my insulated gloves? I swear Saint Christopher is warm, but how, and why?

After landing and having the medics see to Dallas and John we went to debriefing. During debriefing we are offered a shot of whiskey. I always refuse my shot. I guess it's supposed to calm our nerves. A compliment of Uncle Sam. Today was different. I took the whiskey from the Captain and with my hand shaking I drank it all. All meaning what I didn't spill while lifting the glass. Death was so close today.

Returned to *Angel.* She is full of holes. It appears that every square inch of her has taken a beating. Difficult to explain. The bombardier windscreen is gone. Dallas was lucky. The windscreen across the cockpit was shattered to pieces. Several cannon shell holes were visible throughout the nose section. The hole by my navigator table was larger than I thought. How did it miss me?

Dixon was at work. He said two things; the first was, "No other Fortress could have made it back to base." And "It's a miracle. I swear it's a miracle."

Both Dallas and John will be okay. Dallas has a slight wound but John will be in the hospital awhile. Despite all the damage to *Angel* a strange phenomenon has taken place.

Dixon just stares at *Angel.* I can't help but ask him what he is looking at. He doesn't speak; he just looks, in awe, at *Angel.*

Dixon raised his hand and slowly pointed to the painting of *Angel.* The entire area around *Angel's* face has been shot away. It is full of holes. . . But *Angel* hasn't been touched. She remains the same as ever. Peaceful, inspiring and shedding a tear. "What do you make of it?" I asked Dixon.

His answer was ominous and full of contemplation. Hesitating for several seconds he said, “Only God knows.”

* * * * *

Diary, I’m not much of a writer. What I described is not even close to what happened up there today. It was horrifying. Maybe a good writer couldn’t describe it. Maybe it’s beyond words.

* * * * *

God be praised. Just informed we have a weekend pass. I guess they think we need a pass after what happened today. Just enough time to catch the last train from Royston to London. I will see Anne again. God be praised. Dear friend Dixon has agreed to do his best to reach Anne while I rush to the train station. Sergeant Dixon is a genuine friend. We all like him. I hope he finds Anne. If he has luck she will meet me at the London station.

* * * * *

Saint Christopher, you continue to protect me. I pray you will always be by my side. Always. And Thank you, dad, for telling me the story of my protector. I hold him close–I cherish my medal.

JOSEPH DOGLIO AND SAINT CHRISTOPHER

JUNE 1929
THE MAZON RIVER
SOUTH WILMINGTON, ILLINOIS

The two of them, young Joseph Doglio and his father, fished from the grassy bank of the Mazon River. The lazy summer sun provided a picturesque setting for a father and son conversation.

Young Joseph looked across the meandering waters. He pointed to a dark brown snapper turtle as it slowly made its way to a clump of cat tails on the opposite bank.

His father nodded. His six year old son was learning to recognize the signs of nature. Then without warning a sudden splash disturbed the gentle waters.

"What was that?" Joseph asked excitedly.

"Probably some old bluegill or black bass looking for a meal," answered his father.

Joseph's eyes were wide like silver dollars. "Maybe we should move over there," he pointed, "where the fish is."

Albert recognized his son's excitement. The same thing occurred on every fishing trip. There was something about a splash that provided a young boy's imagination to run away with him.

"Well, I guess if we remain patient, sooner or later that old fish will make his way over to where we're sitting." He looked at his son. "What do you think?"

Joseph pondered the question. He searched the river for signs of the mysterious fish. He noticed the reeds moving to his left. On his right he saw a school of minnows scurrying here and there. Probably being pursued by a much larger fish. The sun was partially shaded by the old elm tree that had provided a respite from the heat for many years. His white fishing line began to move. The red and white bobber bounced up and down in a gentle rhythm.

"He's come a callin'," Joseph smiled at his father. "Old fish has come a callin'."

"You bet he has. Now get ready, and when that bobber goes under, you give him time to take the hook and then you pull." Before he could finish telling his son what to do, the red and white bobber disappeared beneath the muddy water. Joseph yanked at his home-made wooden pole, a stick really, and yelled, "I got him, Pa. I got the old rascal."

Albert, as excited as his son, jumped to his feet. "That's it. Hold him tight. Don't let the line loose. Pull him son. By golly, you got him."

The huge fish broke water and leaped through the air. He shook the hook, knowing he was in a fierce battle for survival. The size of the black bass was enormous. Albert couldn't believe his eyes.

"What do I do? What do I do?" Joseph yelled. He's a giant, Pa." The old stick began to bend and the snap of wood was evident. Joseph struggled with his hands to keep the old home-made pole in one piece. "My pole's breakin', Pa. It's breakin' in the middle. Help me, Pa. Help me. Don't let the old fish get away." Joseph fought the old fish and the wooden pole at the same time. He ran to and fro, going where the fish led him. The angry fish broke water again. He seemed to look at his adversary, a small boy, and shook the line in a frenzied fury of fighting power.

Then the sound was heard for miles. At least that was what Joseph would tell his mother. The small pole snapped in two. The broken handle remained in young Joseph's hand while the other half, with old fish attached, slowly sunk beneath the waters.

Father and son stood on the bank staring at a quiet river that showed no sign of the struggle that had just taken place.

Joseph spoke first. "He plum broke my pole, Pa. Old fish broke my pole. He was the biggest fish I ever saw. Probably about twenty pounds, don't you think, Pa?"

"Well, son. . . ."

"Really, Pa. That old fish was like a whale. Golly, wait till I tell ma and Billy. You saw it. Pa. Wasn't he a whale?"

Albert concealed his smile. "He was big son. He sure was big."

"Too big for this little ole river. That's for sure. I said that's for sure. I bet he came here from some giant river somewhere out there and he was just lost. But I got him, Pa. I got him for awhile, anyway." Then he paused to look at the broken pole in his hand. "That old fish beat me, Pa. He beat me fair and square, and I hope he lives to be a hundred years old." His eyes were getting bigger by the minute. "Two hundred years, Pa. He deserves to have a long life. He deserves it."

Joseph's father was taken by the concern in his son's voice. He decided to remain silent for several minutes.

"I want the fish to be okay, Pa. I want him to swim away to some quiet place and nurse his wound. I hurt him, Pa. I must have really hurt him." Joseph looked up and down the river. He looked toward Joyce's farm and then back to his father. "Do fish have other fish who help them? Will old fish find some help?"

Albert stared at the river and then ruffled his son's hair. "I think that old fish can take care of himself. He seemed strong and full of energy. I bet he will be well in no time at all."

"Golly, that may be true, Pa. But what about us? Who protects us when we are traveling down an old lazy river or down an old country road?" Young Joseph was serious and his eyes demanded an answer.

Albert recognized the seriousness in Joseph's voice and in his facial expression. He gave considerable thought to his answer.

"Well, Pa, does someone help us?"

Albert reached for the delicate silver chain that he had worn around his neck since he was a boy. He removed it and showed it to Joseph.

"Do you know what this is, son?"

"I know you wear it every day. I know it's a medal. I don't know why you wear it though."

Albert placed the token and chain in his son's hand. "Here, see this man here?" he pointed at the burly man on the token. "See," he pointed. "He's carrying a child." Joseph examined the huge man and the small child. "Do you know who the child is?" his father asked.

"No, I sure don't, Pa." Joseph studied the token with a child like wonder. "Who is the big man, Pa?"

Albert pointed to the giant of a man and related a story to his son.

"This man, son, is named Saint Christopher. We don't know much about him, but he is one of the Fourteen Holy Helpers. Saint Christopher was a giant of a man, and he wanted to serve the mightiest king on earth."

Joseph moved his fingers across the medal. "Did he?"

"Well, he didn't serve the king because the king was afraid of the devil. He didn't serve the devil because the devil was afraid of the cross, so. . . ."

"So then what did he do?" Joseph was fascinated by his father's story. He moved from one place to another, all the time looking at the medal that hung from the silver chain.

Albert continued, “So the giant of a man sought Christ. That’s what he did.”

“Golly Pa, did he find him, and if he did, how did he do it?” For Joseph, the story was like something his father would tell him before he went to bed. This, he thought, was an added bonus.

“He found him, Joseph. He vowed for the love of Christ to carry travelers on his strong shoulders across a dangerous river. One night, being awakened by a child’s voice calling his name, Saint Christopher hastened to his task. Suddenly, in the midst of the surging waters, the giant who had never stooped beneath the heaviest of weights, was bent down under the burden of this child, grown heavier than the world itself. ‘Be not astonished,’ said the mysterious child, ‘you bear Him who bears the world.’ He then disappeared, blessing his carrier and calling him by his name, Christopher, which means Christ-bearer.”

“Wow, Pa. This giant of a man, Saint Christopher, protects us when we travel. Is that what keeps us safe?”

“We would like to think so, son. If we believe in things, then we can take Saint Christopher with us wherever we go. If something happens to us like something happened to old fish then we can only hope and believe Saint Christopher will take us to a safe place where we have nothing to fear. Ever again."

Young Joseph continued to finger the token. He moved it closer to his eyes and examined the child and the child's protector. Looking at his father he asked, "Can I have a Saint Christopher medal?"

Albert removed the silver chain and token from his son's hand. He unsnapped the clasp and placed the chain around his son's neck. Then he snapped the clasp. Little did he realize that from that moment on Joseph would never remove the medal from his neck.

"It's yours, son." Albert smiled and nodded re-assuredly.

"You mean it, Pa? I can have your Saint Christopher medal?"

"You can son. Let Saint Christopher protect you."

"This is swell, Pa. Wow, I have my own Saint Christopher medal." Joseph stood and walked closer to the river. He placed the medal in his hand and yelled, "Don't worry old fish! Saint Christopher will take care of you, too."

The words no sooner fell across the waters when a giant splash occurred directly in front of Joseph and his father. Joseph's mouth fell open and words could not be found. His father spoke for him.

"I guess Saint Christopher heard you, son. He's taking care of old fish."

"And he'll take care of me, too, Pa. Even in this worst of times."

Joseph looked at the river, and he watched the gentle waters meandering through Joyce's fields, "You take care old fish. You take care."

* * * * *

On July 19, 1944, while a Saint Christopher medal hung from Second Lieutenant Doglio's neck and another hung above his navigators table, a B-17 Flying fortress and her crew met their death.

I assume that on his journey to the land of peace, a land of milk and honey, Joseph was accompanied by a giant of a man who led him home to a heavenly place located far above the universe. Who knows, this giant of a man may have carried

Joseph on his shoulders. Such was Joseph's belief that Saint Christopher would always protect him.

* * * * *

And about the old fish. Well, in his own small way that old fish made Joseph's father a fisher of men.

* * * * *

In 1977, Anne Howard made her journey home. She was no doubt accompanied by a friendly giant. I suspect Anne took the hand of a gentle Saint and she slowly realized the enormity of her journey. She wasn't afraid of the unknown, for her spiritual strength and her willingness to believe were magnified by the Christ-Bearer, Saint Christopher.

* * * * *

Finally, the journey of Anne and Joseph's son was made easier by the sudden appearance of the Saint of Travelers. No words were spoken. The Holy Saint had prepared himself for the arrival of the Royal Air Force pilot. The pilot smiled at the man before him. Reaching for the hand of the kind Saint, Joseph asked, "Will you carry me? I'm tired and I search for a place to rest."

There is no doubt that Saint Christopher obliged.

We know the rest of the story.

THE JOURNAL OF ANNE HOWARD

8 JULY 1944
MORNING
LONDON, ENGLAND

This war is hell on earth! I wish I could kill Adolph Hitler, just twist his evil body into a knot and let the buzzards eat him alive! I know as a Christian, I'm not supposed to think such things, but I can't help it. How is it possible that one person can orchestrate the suffering of so many millions? If anyone deserves a first-class ticket to hell, it's him!

I had the most atrocious dream of my life last night. It was so disturbing that I'd be more than happy to forget it, but I cannot.

I dreamt there was an air raid. Mum, Da and I made our way to the underground shelter to wait for the bombers to pass. As we sat huddled, I happened to notice a small opening in the wall that led to some sort of passageway. Though it was dark, I managed to squirm my way into this little tunnel. I wasn't frightened because I could hear Joey calling out to me from the other end. "I'm coming!" I kept shouting out as I wriggled my way toward the direction of his voice. When I emerged from the tunnel lo and behold, I found myself standing in the middle of a yellow field in Germany. Joey was nowhere to be seen. I looked up into the sky just in time to see a B-17 explode. In one instant the majestic plane shot into flames. I started running as fast as I could through the field, running in the direction of the ground under the explosion. I was out of breath and crying, when I tripped over something and found myself facedown in a pit of death. Oh, diary, I can't tell anyone but you of this nightmare. Some of the bodies in this pit were uniformed, some were completely naked, and all were faceless. God have mercy. I woke myself up crying on the floor next to my bed. Thank God it was only a bad dream!

Needless to say, I was too upset to settle back into any kind of slumber. There can be no true comfort until there is once again peace. I have no greater aspiration in life right now than to see Joey again. My heart sinks a little lower each day that I don't hear from him.

* * * * *

8 JULY 1944

EVENING

My dear, trusty diary—

My prayers have been answered! Joey will be here in London tomorrow. Margaret got the telegram late this afternoon, and apparently he's already caught the last train out of Royston. I am to meet him at London station tomorrow, if I don't crawl out of my skin with excitement before then!

Margaret just left, Mum and I were in the kitchen making tea when she popped in to show me the telegram. I got so excited I picked Margaret up and swung her around me. Mum cast a rather dubious look my way.

"Go ahead and ask Margaret here how fabulous he is, Mum," I said in my giddiness. "She'll tell you!"

So Margaret stayed for tea, and the three of us had a very, shall we say, illuminating chat. Mum loves Margaret like family, and she drilled her for information just as she had me last week during my little confessional with her. I think Margaret helped put Mum's mind at ease; though she said to hear us girls singing such high praises about these Yanks made it difficult for her not to believe that "it's just the war talking. . ."

I'm hoping Joey can come for supper tomorrow evening. Mum's okay with it, but the hardest part will be coaxing Da. I'm prepared to weather the storm. Mum and I will descend upon him after he gets some food in his stomach tonight. Keep your paper fingers crossed, dear diary!

THE JOURNAL OF ANNE HOWARD

9 JULY 1944
LONDON, ENGLAND

I have fallen madly in love, and I no longer have to pretend otherwise. Now that Joey has met Mum and Da, I feel as if a tremendous weight has been lifted from my shoulders. I feel more lighthearted and gay tonight then I've felt in a very long time. I love Joey, and I love Mum and Da, and now they've all met, and, Oh! I'm the most ecstatic girl on the planet!

Joey's train arrived mid-afternoon. I became a bit frantic as the last passengers were leaving the train and still no sign of my love. Then I felt an arm wrap 'round my waist from behind and, though startled, felt my insides begin to melt. My body and mind suddenly afire, I whirled around and did what I've only been able to dream of doing for what has seemed like eons. I could have happily died right there on the spot, in that embrace, an eternal kiss. Oh, to be in his arms again! I'm not sure how long we stood there devouring one another, but it wasn't long enough, dear diary. When we did finally come up for air, both of us were speechless. Joey knelt down and picked up a gorgeous bouquet of burgundy long-stem roses, "for you", he said. "I guess I got a little carried away at seeing you and dropped them." They look so beautiful here next to my bed now, reminding me of my handsome love. . .

We caught a cab and came straight home. I don't know which of us was more anxious about spending the evening with my parents, but Joey insisted he was looking forward to it. I admitted to him that it had taken all of last night to persuade my father; also adding that gaining his approval on most matters was like charming a snake. His initial response is almost always to hit the roof, but eventually he comes 'round. It's his style, and he's honed it for years.

Mum came out to meet us the moment we pulled up. She's so much more resilient than Da, and I knew she would do her best to make everyone – especially Joey – comfortable. "I'm glad to meet you, Lieutenant Doglio. My daughter speaks so highly of you, I'm relieved to see you're made of flesh and blood like the rest of us," she chuckled. "Welcome to our home."

We came inside to find Da hovering over his sherries. Joey and I glanced at one another, as if to say it's now or never. . .

Joey stepped forward to introduce himself, but Da cut him off. "Yes, Lieutenant Doglio, it's my pleasure. Would you care for a sherry?" was what he said. Now Da had promised me that he would be civil, but when he ignored Joey's outstretched hand, I felt the blood rising to my face. Instead of a handshake, a sherry was placed into Joseph's hand. As we all took a seat, I was praying that Da wouldn't embarrass me. . . .

The tone was already set, so naturally it was Da who began directing the conversation. He wanted to know why Joey had joined the Air Corps, what his life had been like back in the States, what his impressions were of England. The conversation went on like this throughout dinner, Da asking Joey questions, and Joey answering in a most respectful manner. I tried several times to divert attention to myself, if for no other reason than to make the atmosphere at the table a bit less disjointed; but Da was relentless. Joey did manage to sneak me a wink across the table at one point, which made my skin tingle. "At least he's been forewarned," I thought to myself.

Thankfully, no questions were asked about our relationship until after dinner. I should have known Da would want to sequester my brave Joey for that line of interrogation, and so he did.

I wasn't able to glean much of what was being said from my position in the kitchen, or from the hallway for that matter, where I was pressed against the wall like a lizard.

When the two of them finally emerged from Da's study, the tension was palpable. Was it too much to ask that Da keep his peevishness under check for one night? I knew he would end up embarrassing me, but poor Joey. . . .

"What were you two discussing in there behind closed doors?" I asked, somewhat feebly.

"Just getting to know one another a little better," Joey offered.

"Well, I do hope father here hasn't managed to scare you away for the rest of the evening."

Mum and I made coffee just now, in your honor. Mum says she's heard how much Americans love their coffee. Please stay awhile. . . ."

And he did stay, dear diary. And the atmosphere thankfully improved. By evening's end, everyone seemed fairly relaxed. Joey even managed to make Da laugh a couple of times, which is no small feat. He likes Joey, I can tell. And I love him (Joey, I mean). I never want this feeling to end! If he asked me to marry him tomorrow, I would! I don't care if it sound naive or foolish; I don't care because I've never been more certain of anything in my life. Tomorrow we will be alone. I'm going to show him Saint George's Church in Anstey. It's there that I'll give him the locket I've placed my picture in. We will say a prayer, and I'll give him the locket. This, I'm hoping with all my might, will keep him safe.

Good night for now. . . .

THE DIARY OF SECOND LIEUTENANT JOSEPH DOGLIO

JULY 9, 1944
LONDON, ENGLAND

I met Anne's family today. Her mother was swell. She did everything she could to make me feel comfortable. Anne's father was completely different. He is suspicious of us (Americans). He honestly thinks we are all bad guys, fighting a war and taking advantage of the women in England. He made his opinions very strong and asked my intentions. Although taken back by his hostility, I held my own. By the end of the evening we actually hit it off.

He told me I could continue to see Anne. But he told me I had to watch my every move. He would not take kindly to me violating Anne in any way. I assured him that was not what I had in mind.

Mrs. Howard served a fine meal. She reminds me of mom. Heaven knows the Howard's must have somehow scraped together enough rationing stamps to serve a meal like that. We even had potatoes and gravy. An English roast, small, but a roast no less. One cup of coffee and a cube of sugar. I hope they will get by until the next stamps are issued. I had no idea Anne was going to do this. I came empty handed.

Anne was excited about the family gathering. She said her father liked me. If he liked me then I'm surely glad he didn't dislike me. But we did seem to do better as the night went along. I said that already. But it was good to see him become friendlier. It was good for Anne and her mother, too.

I said goodnight to Anne with her father looking on. Rather interesting moment, somewhat embarrassing for me but quite humorous to Anne. "Now, now," she whispered in my ear. "No sense acting like a peacock is there now?" Then she giggled. Her father is like a German ME. Ominous, always lurking in the shadows. We will be alone tomorrow. How she takes away my fears. I dare not tell her about the Humieres Mission. She would be devastated.

I'm in love with her. I know I am. I must be. Why else would I feel this way? A thought crossed my mind. If it weren't for this war I wouldn't have met Anne. Maybe that's the only good thing to come of this horrible nightmare called "WORLD WAR II."

Oh, as I walked down the street, away from the Howard home, Anne yelled through the darkened night. She said, "Sleep tight, my handsome Lieutenant." She did that in front of her father. Heaven help me, I thought.

Then her father yelled in his thick English accent. "God be with you, son."

Golly, I was stopped in my tracks. I turned and answered, "And with you, sir."

Sheepishly I acknowledged Anne by bravely saying, "Goodnight now."

Later, walking through a bombed area of London, I began to chuckle. I'm beginning to talk like Anne. Talk like these English folks. "Goodnight now," I sheepishly yelled to Anne. "Goodnight now." In South Wilmington I would have said, "See yah." Oh, Anne, this is so swell.

* * * * *

"God be with you, son." Those were the last words Joseph would hear from Anne's father. Later, he wrote that his memory of that moment made him yearn for a few minutes with his father. One more fishing trip to the winding, muddy waters of the Mazon River.

THE JOURNAL OF ANNE HOWARD

10 JULY 1944
LONDON, ENGLAND

I had almost forgotten how beautiful Saint George's Church is, especially when the sunlight filters in through the stained glass windows. The peacefulness of the place allows you to step out of time for a bit, which is a luxury these days. Joey and I must have sat there in the sanctuary for a good half hour without saying a single word. It was a blessed silence.

Joey asked me if I thought we could spend the rest of our lives right there, "as we are now?" Something was preoccupying his thoughts, that much was evident. My sense was that it had to do with a mission-past or a mission-future, but that either way, he didn't want to talk about it. Rather than trespass upon his thoughts, I asked instead if I might say a prayer aloud for him. I prayed for his crew and his plane *Angel*, and I prayed especially hard that God return him to me after each of his missions. And, as always, I prayed for an end to the war.

Then I gave him my locket. He just sat smiling at it for the longest time, and when he reached out to thank me, there were tears in his eyes. I held him tight in my arms, and we both cried silently. It wasn't what I had expected, but the tears came naturally, and the release felt wonderful.

We left the little sanctuary for the sunshine outside. Roaming about the grounds on the church, we found the shade of a giant oak too enticing to pass by. Here we spent what remained of our day together, locked in an eternal embrace, transcending time and space. . . .

Later, on the train, returning to London, I wrote this letter to Joseph.

My Dearest:

Why must my heart hurt so? Our time together was so brief yet you have left me with memories and feelings, thoughts and embraces, passions and longings. It is hard to imagine that while we are surrounded by such heartache and violence something so beautiful has blossomed between us. But as quickly as you came into my life you left, leaving me with only my thoughts of you to keep me comforted at night. I lie awake wondering where you are and whether you are in danger. Are you thinking of me and loving me with the same intensity that I am for you? I fear that you were a wonderful dream and that soon I must wake up. I don't ever want to wake up! I want this feeling, this yearning inside of me, to never leave.

I can still feel your hand in mine. That gentle way our fingers would intertwine makes me tingle with excitement. You made me come alive inside, igniting a spark that now burns in my heart. A wise man once said, "Absence is to love what wind is to fire; it extinguishes the small but it enkindles the great." The flame in my heart will continue to burn until the moment that I can be with you again and glimpse that smile that made my knees weak, my soul melt, and my whole world brighten.

When our eyes met for the first time, my heart skipped a beat. You stole my heart with only a glance. I long for the day when we can take strolls together at night and gaze up at the twinkling stars without a thought of anything else but one another. I often wonder what it will feel like to hold you in my arms, to kiss you softly and know that we share a bond that not even death can sever. My love for you grows deeper and deeper with each minute that we must be apart. My love knows no other but you and it is deeply rooted in the belief that one day we will be able to be together again, carefree and happy.

I sometimes wonder if one is better off not knowing the wonders of love so that they never have to experience the bitter taste of goodbyes. But then I think of you and I know love is worth all of the pain and sorrow that it inflicts upon the heart. You have given me the gift of perfect love. I find it is easier to laugh and to smile when I think of you because with you I have everything. How is it that I can know you for such a short period of time yet love you with such strong devotion? I will love you always and forever and may the time that I must wait until I can see you again pass quickly.

Love always, Anne

THE JOURNAL OF ANNE HOWARD

19 JULY 1944
LONDON, ENGLAND

A night full of dreams, I can't sleep. I can't distinguish what I'm feeling. Maybe I'm coming down with something. The only activity that brings me any degree of peace is writing to you, dear diary. Even at half past three in the morning, you're able to listen. . . .

Something feels out of place. My head is clear, yet my thoughts somehow don't add up. I feel as if I've been anesthetized, and I must be sounding as if I'm crazy.

The house is so quiet right now. I long for daylight. Each morning brings with it the promise of a letter or telegram from Joey. Perhaps today will be the day. I miss him so much!

* * * * *

As Anne wrote in her journal, her precious Joseph prepared for his last mission.

THE DIARY OF SECOND LIEUTENANT JOSEPH DOGLIO

JULY 19, 1944 NUTHAMPSTEAD, ENGLAND

THE LAST ENTRY

0315 hours. Target must be Germany. I feel strong today. No reason for this strength. Funny, but in a way it's a different kind of strength. Something from within has filled my body. My senses are consumed by a restful, almost serene feeling. I can't put my finger on this emotion. I feel a pleasure. That's it. I feel a pleasure. It's as though I have been washed clean of this war. My mind is free. It's as though I too can fly. Fly like our Angel, but today I don't need her. Today I have the strength to ascend to the pinnacle of the sky.

Just learned the target is an airfield in Lechfeld, Germany. Mission number eleven. No jitters this morning. This inner strength continues to embrace my mind. God help me explain this. I am calm, almost carefree. Amongst the early morning preparations for number eleven I am amazed with this spiritual peacefulness. I have never before encountered this incredible experience.

We are on our way to *Angel.* Dixon, as usual, is behind the wheel of the Jeep. O'Neill just surprised us. He actually asked that God be with us today. He's never said anything like that before. He has this thing about religion. We were all shocked by his wishes. He, Schultz, and Cosco are not flying today.

I asked Earl if he felt different. He gave me a strange and puzzling look. He nodded, yes. I asked if he felt strong, at peace. He nodded again. Earl doesn't speak but he, too, seems calm. His steps are not taken with an anticipation of what is to come during this mission to Germany. Instead he moves as though he is going home, to Marion, Virginia.

Father Sullivan gave us communion. I turned to Dallas. He was saying something to Dixon, "You've been a good friend."

When they finished talking I took Dallas by the arm, "Do you feel different today?"

His eyes focused on me. Then he turned and walked to our *Angel*, our Fortress. He took Dixon's engine ladder and climbed to the painting of her face. His hand moved slowly across the beautiful artwork. He brushed at *Angels* tear. I can't take my eyes off him. My eyes are fixed on this proud pilot as well our beautiful, delicate, and always forgiving Flying Fortress. Suddenly he yells down, "Joseph, I have the feeling this will be our best flight. I just have this feeling."

I asked Dixon to take Anne's locket. I'm giving him my diary. I have asked him to keep it safe and if something happens to me, I have given him Anne's address.

My God, my inner strength is beyond words. Saint Christopher, protect me. If necessary, take me home. Take our *Angel* home.

I love you, Anne!

I love you, mom and dad! Another mission. I'll be brave, mom. Like a lion.

Anne, this feeling! What can it mean? I embrace this feeling as though I am embracing you. It's like heaven. Strength, beauty, carefree, and this spiritual pleasure; I am at peace in your arms, Anne.

They say there is peace in heaven. Are you from heaven? Were you heaven's gift to me?

* * * * *

On July 19, 1944, the B-17 Flying Fortress named *Angel* and her crew departed Base 131, Nuthampstead, England, at 0600 hours (British time). They carried fifty, one hundred pound Incendiary bombs. John Cosco, William Schultz, and Carroll O'Neill, original members of the *Angel* crew, were replaced by substitutes John Loomis, Gordon Sudborough, and Gregory Gronki. The target was an airfield located near Lechfeld, Germany. At 0955 hours, German time, the *Angel* received two direct hits from a German Flak Battery located in Scheuring, Germany. The left wing of *Angel* was torn from the plane while the fuselage of *Angel* broke into two parts. The waist gunner was the sole survivor.

The remains of the *Angel* crew were found buried, at the Wolfgang-Chapel, near Weil at Landsberg/Lech,Germany. The remains were discovered in 1948.

THE JOURNAL OF ANNE HOWARD

9 AUGUST 1944
LONDON, ENGLAND

I'm sorry I've been neglecting you, my dear diary. The only excuse I have is that I've been throwing myself into work at the Admiralty, as this is the only method I have of controlling my growing anxiety over Joey's well-being. Surely over the course of a solid month he would have found the time to write me even the briefest note. He knows how much I worry about his safety. The worst is that Margaret hasn't heard anything from Earl, either. I'm terribly afraid something is wrong. These feelings of uncertainty and helplessness are absolute torment. I have resolved to investigate the matter if I haven't received word from him by week's end. I'm trying to keep optimistic, but under such circumstances, it's proving to be the greatest challenge of my life.

THE JOURNAL OF ANNE HOWARD

26 AUGUST 1944
MORNING
LONDON, ENGLAND

Never before have I felt so all alone. The days drag by, empty and meaningless. I've scarcely left my room in a fortnight. Last week I even refused to take shelter during an air raid, thoroughly upsetting Mum and Da. I suppose it was childish of me, but at the time I honestly wanted to die. Go ahead and take me, too, bloody war – you've left me with no reason to live. . .

On 12 August, my worst fear was confirmed. Joseph was killed during a bombing mission over Germany. It pains me even now to write those words, and thus to see them written by my own hand – as if doing so only adds to the finality of my loss.

Margaret and I went to the Nuthampstead Air Base to get some answers that day. Thank God Margaret agreed to go with me. The guard at the gate put us in touch with a

Father Walter Sullivan. When I saw a chaplain had been sent for, I thought I might faint. He took us to his office. He said something about regulations requiring he ask what my relationship was to Joey, which seemed agonizingly rude. Then he was next to me saying those horrible things that couldn't be true. Wasn't there some chance a mistake had been made? Then he was holding my hand, saying something about God's will. . . . He tried to be delicate, that chaplain, but it didn't really matter how he said it. He might just as well have driven a stake through my heart. My memory is blurry after that. Somehow, dear Margaret got me home. I've been here ever since.

I've re-played every single moment Joey and I shared together, trying to find a clue, some sign, that he knew what the future had in store. Over and over, I re-live those moments – scanning them, dissecting them, reducing myself to a puddle of tears. Somehow, I feel there is more dignity in a person sensing their own fate, as if God or an angel were reaching out a hand to reassure and guide you. I cannot bear the thought of him suffering in any way. My one prayer is that God took him mercifully. I just can't believe he is gone. Please, God, help me to understand. . . .

* * * * *

26 AUGUST 1944

EVENING

Margaret stopped by for a visit this afternoon. She's organizing a little soiree for my birthday next week. How in the world she thinks I'll be able to socialize at a time like this is beyond me. I begged her please not to go to the trouble, but she's already invited people. I'm afraid I'll break down in front of her guests. "Nonsense," she tells me, "you underestimate yourself." She and Mum both insisted that I can't very well stay cooped up in my room forever. I told her I'd do my best to be there. "Oh, you'll be there, alright," she says, "even if I have to come and drag you by your heels!" Typical Margaret. . . .

I realize I can't change what has happened; nor can I hide from the reality of it. I only want to make sense of it all. Why were Joey and I allowed to meet at all, if he was only going to be snatched away so abruptly? Was his death a horrid accident, or is fate a cruel and capricious force directing our lives? I feel as if I was made to stand ten feet tall, only to have the rug yanked swiftly out from under my feet. How can I make sense of this? And yet how can I heal and move on if I don't? I think of the last hours we shared together, basking in our love for one another. It seemed endless. I've never felt so completely fulfilled. . . .

How painfully hard it was to part with him that day in Anstey. How much more painful now is my recollection of it. To think of his strong warm body now lifeless and cold. . .

How can I make sense of this? I believed my love could protect him. . . Giving him my locket was my guarantee that he return safely to me after each mission. Were you wearing it, my dear Joseph? Did giving you the locket have any significance at all, or was it just a naive, meaningless gesture?? If only I could believe it mattered. . . . If only I could be given some kind of sign. . . . When you promised me you'd be with me always, I believed you. What am I to make of that promise now?

THE JOURNAL OF ANNE HOWARD

3 SEPTEMBER 1944
EVENING, ANNE'S BIRTHDAY
LONDON, ENGLAND

Margaret's plan to get me out of the house worked. The evening out proved to be quite a tonic after all. I actually feel invigorated for the first time since last I saw Joey, my love. I've had time to sort out my feelings. I understand that life is full of unexpected twists and turns, disappointments and surprises. It seems these are especially trying times, when outside events almost completely consume the personal details, eating away at that we most cherish. Such is war, to the utmost degree. Yet there is always a stone or two left unturned, a secret chamber of the soul where we go to wrought meaning. Tonight I finally understand Joey's promise to me. Our promise to each other. I'm no longer confused. I'm no longer alone. . . .

ANNE'S BIRTHDAY

3 SEPTEMBER, 1944

LATE EVENING

LONDON, ENGLAND

THE UNTURNED STONE AND JOSEPH'S PROMISE

* * * * *

ANNE HOWARD AND SERGEANT MARK DIXON

Sergeant Dixon waited in the darkened street. The rain had progressed from a slow, steady drizzle to periods of constant downpours. He found himself huddled against a grayish building which posted a sign, "Teddy's Bakery". Looking through the dirty gray windows he realized the bakery had been closed for sometime. Not just weeks, but obviously for months.

He had been waiting for several hours and now, at 10:45, he was throughly drenched. His military raincoat was no longer protecting him. Now the water logged raincoat held the cold moisture against his body. He began to feel a chill.

Sergeant Dixon, despite the torrential rain, had no thoughts of leaving. Earlier he had located the Howard home and learned from Anne's parents that Anne was attending a birthday party in her honor. It was Mr. Howard who addressed Dixon.

"She's been beside herself, Sergeant. It seems her very life has been taken from her. She lives and breathes, she forces herself to go to the Admiralty, but heaven knows she has lost her will to live." He paused to contemplate his next words. "Her heart is beating, you see, but it provides the blood and not the spirit. Her spirit is dead. It's gone." Shaking his head, slowly his saddened eyes found the floor beneath him.

Mrs. Howard held her husband's hand. "Sergeant, today is Anne's birthday. Her friend Margaret is having a party for her. She wouldn't go, mind you. She refused and threw a tantrum! But between the three of us we convinced her to at least give it a try. I'm afraid we should have left it well enough alone."

Sergeant Dixon was uncomfortable. He spoke in generalities and then he told them why he was there.

"I have a letter for Anne, your daughter. Lieutenant Doglio wrote it the day before his final mission. He asked that I give it to her." He realized the enormity of what he was saying. "I'm sorry, but I believe Joseph, Lieutenant Doglio, felt uneasy about his last mission. You could see it in his eyes. The whole crew was unsettled."

"Do you think they knew?" Mr. Howard asked.

"I don't know sir, but the *Angel* crew was different. They were swell kids. All of them." The Sergeant hesitated for a moment and solemnly added. "I don't believe they received what had been promised. God, I believe, had planned something far greater. Maybe one day I'll find the answers to my questions."

There was an uneasy pause in the conversation.

"We can take the letter, if you wish," Mrs. Howard said looking from Dixon to her husband.

Mr. Howard nodded, "We'll see she gets it."

Sergeant Dixon thanked them and politely answered, "Thank you, but I promised my friend I would give it to your daughter personally. I've not met Anne, but perhaps if you told me where she might be, I'll find the address and," he paused, taking a deep breath, "and give it to her myself. I'm sure you understand."

Having found the building on Abbington Circle, he waited in the rain. The letter remained in his kit, safe from the London weather.

Suddenly a door from across the street opened. Two women stood in the foyer of the building. They talked for several moments, and then they embraced for what seemed an eternity. A few more words were exchanged before Anne Howard walked to the sidewalk and into the driving rain.

Moving toward her, Sergeant Dixon beckoned, "I'm sorry, but by chance are you Anne Howard?" He felt awkward and totally aware that he had frightened her.

Startled, Anne moved away. She didn't answer the stranger, instead she turned to make her way back to Margaret's apartment.

"Miss Howard, I'm terribly sorry." Sergeant Dixon followed her, "My name is Dixon, Sergeant Mark Dixon. I'm a friend of Lieutenant Doglio's."

Anne stopped and turned toward him. The rain was relentless but somehow neither of them could feel it. Their eyes were locked together, exploring each other, until Anne broke the silence.

"Joey spoke of you." It was all she could say.

"Yes ma'am, well, I've waited across the street," he pointed to the empty bakery. "I have something for you, Miss Howard. Perhaps we could go somewhere where it's dry. I'm afraid what I have would be ruined by this terrible rain."

Anne was feeling more comfortable. "Oh, forgive me. Just look at you. You are practically drowning." She took his hand and led him to Margaret's apartment. There they stood under the small roof which lent some protection from the rain.

Sergeant Dixon spoke first. "He wrote a letter to you, Miss Howard. I have it here, in my kit." He reached inside his waterlogged raincoat. Handing it to her he continued. "He gave it to me before his last mission. Said if anything happened I was to give it to you, personally. I'm sorry Miss Howard, but this is my first leave since Joseph was. . . ."

Anne looked at the letter and then to Sergeant Dixon. Despite the rain he could see the tears welling in her eyes. She was everything Joseph said. He was taken by her easy sense of kindness and the warmth that seemed so evident in her facial expressions. He thought there was a passive beauty about her. Not made up, but a beauty so uncommon that it emanated from her eyes and her smile.

"Well, that's it then," Dixon said. "I'll be on my way. Miss Howard, if you want to talk about Joseph, Lieutenant Doglio, you can reach me at the base. Just ask for Sergeant Dixon. They'll find me."

Brushing her hand across her face, Anne took his hand. "You must come in. Please. You're soaking wet. Heaven knows you'll be deathly ill if you don't dry off." She turned toward the door just as it opened.

"Well, what do we have here?" It was Charles Spencer from the Admiralty. "Is this Yank bothering you, Anne?"

"Charles," Anne answered, "this is Sergeant Mark Dixon. Sergeant Dixon was assigned to *Angel.* He was Joseph's ground crew chief." Then turning to Sergeant Dixon, she introduced Charles Spencer.

Dixon extended his hand. Spencer hesitated and then moved toward him and offered a handshake. Dixon had an immediate reaction to the stranger. He felt uneasy with him. A matter of distrust. His instincts were usually correct.

Turning to Anne, he nodded and apologized, "Thank you, Miss Howard, but I think I'll be on my way. I'm to meet some friends and I'm afraid I'm quite late."

"But Sergeant Dixon, you're. . . ."

"I'm wet," he laughed, "but I'll be fine." Before leaving he added, "You know where to find me."

Anne and Charles watched Dixon turn the corner. "I'll drive you home. I won't allow you to refuse this time. The weather is dreadful." Charles took her hand.

"I must go inside. Please Charles, give me a moment will you?"

She made her way to Margaret's bedroom. Closing the door she moved her hand across the envelope. She couldn't control her emotions. In her hand were Joseph's last words to her. It was more than she could bear. Slowly she opened the envelope.

Anne:

A strange feeling has overcome me. I can't explain this feeling as it is most marvelous and yet most unsettling. Unable to understand these moments, I am convinced I must write to you.

My hand nor my mind know not what to write or what to say, so I rely entirely on my heart to find the proper words.

Anne, tomorrow's mission will no doubt be my last. It is a feeling, but I cannot dismiss it from my mind. If it is indeed my last mission, then you must know that I love you. I will forever love you and I will eagerly await your presence in some far off place, a truly magnificent place, that we will someday call home.

Until that time, I promise to look after you as best I can. I'm sure there is a way. Some unturned stone somewhere in the great Heavens will provide me with the answer.

I am embarrassed to say this to you, but under the circumstances I would be remiss if I did not tell you my dreams and how I sheepishly hid them from you.

Our time together will remain with me forever. I promise you that. And Anne, please remember that our last time together was the happiest. I have no need to explain. We both know what we felt and how the feeling remains in our hearts. Remember how I saw you off at the Royston Station. With tears in my eyes I kissed you and waved goodbye as you leaned out the window as the train steamed off.

As the trained pulled away I memorized your face. Every feature from your eyes, your mouth, your beautiful flowing hair. The picture of that moment will be forever painted in my mind.

The train, and you, disappeared from view. As I stood, alone, with your locket in hand, your face in my memory, I thought of the words of Frances Tompson:

She went and left
In me the memory
Of all the partings gone
And partings yet to be. . . .

Do you understand,

Anne? Do you. . . .

God, I love you.

Remember me,

Joseph

Silence filled the room. The soft patter of rain against the window broke the quiet of the moment. The dim light was like a ray of hope that suddenly reached for her. Anne returned the letter to the envelope from whence it came. She studied her name on the face of the gray covering. She studied his writing.

A smile came to her face. She whispered to herself and perhaps to the ray of light that touched her hands and the small gray envelope.

"No Joseph, I'll not forget our last time together. Never!"

Anne walked to the window. She turned off the light before opening the blackout curtains. She studied the street and the falling rain. A thought crossed her mind. An unsettling thought.

"How do I keep my promise?"

She opened the door. Charles Spencer was waiting.

THE JOURNAL OF ANNE HOWARD

BIRTH DATE
LONDON, ENGLAND

DATE:_May 15, 1945 Joseph Earl Howard is born.

Amid the ceaseless agony and peril of war, I have had the greatest blessing of all bestowed upon me. Though there's no question the last year has been the most difficult time of my life, today is the culmination of joy. Gazing into your little pink, wrinkled face, I feel for the first time endowed with a sense of purpose. My baby boy! You shall be named Joseph Earl Howard! One day I'll have quite a story to tell you. . . . My little Joseph, born of pure and perfect love. A promise made and kept. A reason to have hope. You will come to know your father through me. Silently, he will help me raise you into a man. A man perhaps like he was. I've never been so proud! I've also never been so exhausted!

THE HOME OF MR. AND MRS. ALBERT DOGLIO

DECEMBER 1947
SOUTH WILMINGTON, ILLINOIS USA

The following letter was found neatly folded in Anne Howard's journal. Anne Howard's response to this letter is found in the following chapter.

* * * * *

December 6, 1947

South Wilmington, Illinois

Dear Miss Howard:

Forgive us for writing, as you may not wish to hear from us. We found a reference of you in our son's (Joseph) personal effects. He seemed to think very highly of you and as such we are curious if you can tell us how you and our son became acquainted? If you find this to be an unreasonable request we will perfectly understand your reluctance to answering our inquiry. As you might well know, it has been three and one-half years since our Joseph's death and we are continuing to wait for any word as to where he might have been laid to rest. It is as though he suddenly disappeared from the face of the earth. We are anxious to know more about his time in England and how he lived his last days. Perhaps you can shed some light on his life during May, June, and July 1944.

We know this letter could very well be returned to us as the war has taken a heavy toll on civilians and soldiers alike. If this is the case then we will assume our search for answers must be turned elsewhere.

It is our sincere hope that this letter reaches you and that you are in good health.

Kindest personal regards,

Mr. And Mrs. Albert Doglio

ANNE HOWARD'S APARTMENT

JANUARY 26, 1948
LONDON, ENGLAND

The following letter from Anne Howard to Mr. and Mrs. Doglio was found attached to the letter received from Joseph's parents. It is not known if a copy of this letter was ever sent to the Doglio family.

* * * * *

January 26, 1948

London, England

Dearest Mr. And Mrs. Doglio,

Your precious letter arrived just yesterday. I read it over and over until I totally memorized your every word. My heart continues to beat with excitement.

You must forgive me as I find it difficult to write my feelings. So for now perhaps I will simply tell you that I indeed knew your son, Joseph.

You can be very proud of your son as he was a brave navigator and he was revered and respected by his crew. He was every bit a gentleman and the finest person I have ever known. He changed my life forever and I, as you, miss him dearly. Words, I'm afraid, cannot express my desire to have him near me.

You must know, that I too, have tried to find Joseph but despite the efforts of several friends at the Admiralty I seem to have had little success.

Please know that when I collect myself I will write again, soon. Joseph spoke of you in such loving ways. He loved you will all his heart.

Sincerely,

Anne Howard

PS: I have been reluctant to write you for all these painful years. I was so afraid you might not approve of me prying into this dreadful and personal family matter.

POINT OF INTEREST

JUNE 18, 2001
FORT MYERS BEACH, FLORIDA USA

The *Angel* crew was shot down by a German flak position on July 19, 1944. Four years later, on August 12, 1948, Albert Doglio, Joseph's father, sent the following letter to the office of the Quartermaster General.

Although the letter is polite and to the point, one must only imagine the frustration and anxiety suffered by the Doglio family. After four long years there remained no clue as to the whereabouts of their son.

Thus the following letter. . .

* * * * *

South Wilmington, Illinois

August 12, 1948

Office of the Quartermaster General

Dear Sirs:

In reference to your file QMGMS "293", Doglio, Joseph D., SN 0-717191. After four long years of waiting, we received your letter of July 15th, 1948. We have received very little information, and very little personal effects, and sometimes we wonder.

If you have anything in your files in regards to the identification of our son, or other information my wife and I would greatly appreciate it.

Hoping you can give us a little more enlightenment.

I remain yours very truly,

/s/Albert Doglio

South Wilmington, Illinois

* * * * *

Again, another point of interest.

On September 5, 1948, the Doglio family received the following letter from Major James F. Smith, QMC, Memorial Division.

For the first time in four years the search for Second Lieutenant Joseph Doglio, navigator of *Angel*, was revealing some very important clues.

The long ordeal was finally coming to an end.

* * * * *

31 August 1948

Mr. Albert Doglio

South Wilmington, Illinois

Dear Mr. Doglio:

Your letter of 12 August 1948 requesting information relative to the identification of your son has been received. Your request is most understandable, and I shall be only too happy to comply.

Army Air Force records of missing aircraft contain a report on your son's plane. According to this report, this B-17g aircraft, No. 42-102511 was lost near Lechfeld, Germany, 19 July 1944, at 9:54 A.M. Eight of the crew including Joseph were killed and one man captured.

Official German records now on file in this office include a report on the "downing" of a Boeing Fortress II, B-17g, #2102511, on 19 July 1944 at 10:30 A.M., 2KM Northwest of Weil, Germany. This report contained a list of "dog tags", including your son's, "Joseph D. Doglio 0717191 T 42-440C". This report further stated that the dead were buried in three coffins by the community of Weil.

The remains which have been identified as those of your son were recovered from the Civilian Cemetery of Weil. The identification was based on the following:

1. *Tooth chart of this deceased compared almost identically with your son's Army dental records, and did not compare with records of other crew members not yet identified.*
2. *Army Air Force and Official German records in agreement.*
3. *Remains recovered from Weil Civilian Cemetery together with those of three others positively identified, and four tentatively identified as members of your son's crew.*
4. *The cemetery records indicate the only Americans buried in this cemetery are from aircraft #42-102511.*

Your inquiry concerning the personal effects of your son will be the subject of a further communication.

It is my hope that the above information will tend to alleviate your anxiety. Permit me to extend to you and Mrs. Doglio my sincere sympathy in your great loss.

Sincerely yours,

JAMES F. SMITH

Major, QMC

Memorial Division

* * * * *

The initial clue of the burial of the *Angel* crew came in the form of a certified letter dated May 28, 1946. The letter was signed by RILL, Burgermeister, of Weil, Germany. His certified letter was filed in the records of the US Army. Later, the remains of Joseph Doglio were buried at the US Military Cemetery in St. Avold, France. At the time of burial the remains of the crewmembers were listed as UNKNOWN. While the Doglio family waited for word of their son he was laid to rest in plot X, row 9, grave #101 in St. Avold.

A copy of the certified letter from the Burgermeister is as follows: (German and translation)

Ort: Weil

Kreis: Landsberg

Regierungsbezirk: Ober-Bayern

BESCHEINIGUNG

Es wird heirmit bescheinigt, dass im Friedhof der Gemeinde Weil 7 amerikanische Soldaten beeridgt waren, die bei einem Flugzeugabsturz am 19.7 .1944 ums Leben gekommen waren.

Die Leichen der 7 amerikanischen Soldaten wurden am 28. 5.46 ausgegraben und abgenholt.

Weil, den 28.5.46

RILL Burgermeister

CERTIFICATE

This is to certify, that in the cemetery of Weil, were buried 7 American Deceased. The Plane Crash was on 19 July 1944.

The Deceased of 7 American Soldiers were removed on 28 May 1946.

Weil, 28 May 1946

RILL Burgermeister

A CERTIFIED TRUE COPY.

ROBERT M.MAINES

2nd Lt. INF. 689 1st QM.GR.CO (Prov)

POINT OF INTEREST

FEBRUARY 18, 1949
THE RETURN OF JOSEPH DOGLIO'S EFFECTS
SOUTH WILMINGTON, ILLINOIS USA

Nearly five years after Joseph's death, a wooden crate arrived at the Doglio home in South Wilmington, Illinois. Attached to the light brown crate was a simple notification that the enclosed contents were the personal effects of Second Lieutenant Joseph D. Doglio.

The sudden and unexpected appearance of these personal belongings had a traumatic affect on Albert and Kate Doglio. These personal belongings were all that remained of their son's memories.

An inventory of these personal belongings, as returned by the United States government, are listed below:

1 kit containing 10 bars of soap; 1 roll of film; 1 whistle; 6 pkgs. of gum; 1 Blitz cloth; 3 shoe polish; 1 razor; 1 brush holder; 2 buckles; 1 belt; 1 bracelet; 10 boxes razor blades; 1 pill bottle; 1 rosary; 1 shoe brush; 3 spools of

thread; 2 US Air Corps insignias; 1 gold locket; 1 Lt. Bar; 2 shoe laces; 1 tooth brush; 1 lipstick; 1 game of checkers; 1 can cover; 2 pr. gloves; 2 protractors; 1 testament; 1 pocketbook containing misc. letters; 1 service cap and insignia; 1 pr. P.T. shoes; 1 pr. house shoes; 1 pr. service shoes; 1 pr. oxford w/tree; 1 field jacket; 1 khaki shirt; 1 pr. P.T. trunks; misc. papers; 1 bundle of dry cleaning; 1 pink shirt; and 1 pr. green trousers.

A US Army clerk, by the name of Fedeli, inventoried the above items.

PLEASE NOTE THAT ITEM NUMBER EIGHTEEN (18) IS A GOLD LOCKET. IT IS NOT KNOWN IF THIS WAS THE LOCKET GIVEN TO JOSEPH BY ANNE HOWARD. NOR IS IT KNOWN IF THIS IS THE LOCKET THAT WAS MYSTERIOUSLY RETURNED TO ANNE HOWARD IN ANSTEY, ENGLAND ON JULY 19, 1955.

THE JOURNAL OF ANNE HOWARD

6TH BIRTHDAY
LONDON, ENGLAND

It's hard to believe my precious child is six years old today. I think of him sleeping now: tucked safely in his blankets; his moist, sweet breath hovering just over his face; dreaming, no doubt, of airplanes. Only six years of age, and already he talks of being a pilot someday. I must say his father has an unequivocal manner of allowing his influence to be felt. This fascination with the sky is pure Joey. How I do miss him. .

Sometimes I feel selfish for raising Joseph alone, without the presence of a father-figure. It seems unfair to him. As curious and fearless as he already is, I worry that I might not be able to keep up with him! I vow to do my best, though, because this is the only way. There is only one man little Joseph will ever call father. The idea of a surrogate is out of the question, unthinkable. And like his father, I know in my heart that my boy will test life to the limit. It frightens me to admit this, since naturally I wish to protect him always from harm. Yet it is the inevitability of this drive he possesses, this fearlessness, that ties everything together to create meaning in both of our lives. It is the continuing strand. Yes, this bravery is his precious inheritance from his father, and it will be the force that shapes his destiny. It is my duty to swallow my own fear and make sure his path remains unobstructed. There really is no other way. I must raise Joseph Earl alone. To do otherwise would be a travesty. Someday he will understand.

MAY 1975

THE NORTH SEA

The Saint Christopher medal, as it had for years, dangled from the air intake lever of the Royal Air Force Jaguar GRIB Fighter-Bomber. The religious token, given to him shortly after birth, was worn and aged. At times he had an impulse to replace it, but the meaning of its role in his life would not allow Joseph Earl Howard to part with something so special. Special to his mother and to himself.

"Ah, Coltishall, this is Jaguar ADGB, *Angel,* do you read?"

"Ah, Roger, *Angel.*"

"Jolly good then. I have some weather developing to my North," he paused for an instrument check, "I'm going to swing around the nasty stuff. Heading for home."

"Roger, *Angel.* Stay in touch ole man. Wouldn't want you to neglect us."

A smile crossed his face. "Pip, pip an all that. Keep dinner warm, will you."

Signing off, he banked his *Angel* away from the threatening weather. The bright sun in the southern sky reflected against the mass of clouds giving them an ominous look of blues and blacks. "Evil looking storm," he muttered.

The sun, for a brief second, reflected off the Saint Christopher medal. He had become familiar with the occasional glow of his patron Saint. There were times when he actually convinced himself that Saint Christopher really did protect him. He had heard the stories from his mother and someday, he promised himself, he would delve into the mysteries that surrounded his family.

Once again he scanned the instrument panel. Air speed, 680 MPH, altitude 26,000 feet. His two Turbomeca/Rolls Royce Adour turbo fans were taking him home, back to England from another AAR practice mission. The air to air refueling completed, he found himself relaxed, and looking forward to a weekend with his mother.

The Jaguar began to distance itself from the voluminous clouds to the North. He penciled co-ordinates and times on his knee chart before checking with Coltishall.

Suddenly, without warning, his controls felt bulky and a vibration swept through the cockpit. The warning alarm pierced his ears as the red flame out light illuminated the instrument panel.

The Jaguar began to shutter. He pressed the ignition switch. Nervously he waited for a response. Not receiving a reaction he tried again.

"Jolly well. C'mon. C'mon *Angel.*" He felt the perspiration gathering on his brow. The air speed indicator was falling off rapidly. "Not much time, blast it," he cursed under his breath.

He hit the ignition switch again. He felt the pressure against his finger. The pressure seemed to pass through the weather protective gloves on his hand.

"Steady, Joseph. Steady, old boy." He had little time left to make a decision. In a few seconds his loss of airspeed would take him in a spiral toward the North Sea.

"May Day. May Day. Ah, Coltishall do you read."

"We have you *Angel.*"

"I have a flame out. I'm ejecting. I'll need ASR. Tell them to bloody well get a move on."

Before hearing a response the Jaguar slipped into a dizzy, spiraling spin toward the water below. The gravitational force pulled at his body. His lungs were desperately reaching for air. He felt the darkness claiming his mind. Trying to keep control of his senses, he knew it was too late.

"*Angel*, do you read me? Talk to me, Joey." A pause, "Joey, talk to me." Turning to his command center partner, the radar officer calmly uttered, "I've lost Joey."

"I have a May Day," the officer barked. He reported *Angel's* coordinates to Air-Sea Rescue. "Advise."

Air Sea Rescue responded, "We're on our way. Give us updates, will you?"

Joseph managed to reach for the token. He was slipping away but somehow, someway he had to touch the medal. His eyes focused on the glowing face of Saint Christopher. The sun seemed to give this gentle Saint an eerie glow. He saw his mother's face and he saw the face of a World War II hero. The face of a man he had not met. The face of a man he adored. A man he had admired as if he had known him all his life.

Then, as if by some miracle, with the sea just seconds away, his *Angel* came to life. The Turbomeca/Rolls Royce turbo fans began to breath life into the Jaguar. He tried to reach for the controls but the gravitational force would not let go.

Suddenly, as if by some Divine hand, his *Angel* found peace with the sky. The shuddering faded away. The shaking of the fuselage gave way to an angelic smoothness. A gentleness seemed to caress his body. Joseph's hands began to function, his mind was alert; he took control of *Angel.*

His eyes swept across the instrument panel. To his surprise all systems were normal, and more surprisingly, his Jaguar was on a direct course for Coltishall. It was, Joseph thought, as if some unseen navigator who was familiar with the North Sea had set a course for home; home across the wintery cold waters.

Steadying himself, gaining more control of his actions, he looked at his right hand. To his astonishment he continued to clutch the Saint Christopher medal. A shiver ran through his body. Joseph turned his head to face the bright sun in the heavens. The blue sky along with the glowing sun seemed to speak to him. An eternity seemed to pass.

"Ah, Coltishall, this is Jaguar ADGB." A tear gathered in the corner of his eye. Slowly the tear made its way down his cheek. The tear seemed to linger. Joseph Earl Howard brushed at it with his flight glove. The tear remained. He brushed at it again, more vigorously this time. Joseph felt a surge of emotion. He looked at his glove. He saw the dampness on the fibers. The warmth passed through the material and seemed to touch his skin.

At that moment he realized it was all true. The mysteries were now a part of his life.

Joseph gathered himself and once again spoke to Coltishall.

"This is Jaguar ADGB. This is *Angel.* Do you read me?"

* * * * *

Second Lieutenant Joseph Doglio had kept his World War II promise. He vowed the North Sea would never claim the life of a Doglio.

THE HOME OF
JOSEPH AND ALYSSA HOWARD

OCTOBER 4, 1977
COLTISHALL, ENGLAND

The journal, of his mother, remained on Joseph's night stand. The passing of his mother continued to weigh on his mind. He noticed his thoughts wandering as he flew his Jaguar through the English skies. Not a good thing for him to do. Flying a Jaguar at speeds in excess of seven hundred miles per hour demanded his undivided attention. He placed his hand on the journal. His fingers moved gently across the aged leather cover.

"Joseph. Please. Why don't you open it?" Alyssa moved closer. "If nothing else perhaps you can read the first page. Just one page. It's a beginning, you know." She pleaded with him, "Don't you understand she wanted you to read it."

Joseph turned his back to her. "I somehow think this is her private journal. It must be so personal." He turned to face Alyssa. "You know what I mean, sweetie? This is her life story." He smiled, "Maybe there are things I don't want to know."

Placing his hands on the shoulder of his wife he continued, "There is so much I don't know about mom, and yet what I do know is all so beautiful. I have this awkward feeling that this journal belongs to my mother and neither me, nor you, or anyone in this world has the right to open something that is so private, so personal, and for that matter, well, confidential. These words are her memories." He paused again, thinking, "Well, maybe Margaret. She knew mom best."

Alyssa returned his earlier smile, " Oh, for Gods sake, Joseph Earl Howard. There are times when you are so noble, so idealistic; she wanted you to read her journal. Why can't you get that through your thick skull?"

She lifted the journal from the night stand. "Here. Page one. Read it."

"You are one damn persistent woman," he said, taking the journal, fumbling with the pages as he reluctantly began to read.

23 June 1944

This day has been like a dream!! I've kept pinching myself to see if I'd wake up!! My day at the Admiralty. . .

He continued to read in silence. Alyssa looked at him. Her eyes were inquiring. They spoke to him with a woman's curiosity.

That's when I first noticed him. Joseph.

His eyes went from the journal to Alyssa. A grin crossed his face. "This first entry. It's about mom's first meeting with my father. It's so amusing and yet so beautiful."

He handed her the journal. "Read from the beginning, down to here," pointing to the sentence where he had ended.

She read the beginning, stopping where he had pointed. Then slowly in her soft voice she began to read as if Anne Howard herself was reading her own words.

. . . He didn't see me looking at him right away, but before I could break my stare, our eyes locked. . .

Alyssa read the entire entry. When she finished, she gently closed the pages of Anne's journal.

"Joseph, it's precious." Alyssa's voice was so understanding. "She was so young, so innocent, and yet you can feel her emotion. There is a certain joy to her words. So pristine and yet at that moment so alive with curiosity." Pausing, "Your father must have been very handsome in his uniform. Oh, Joseph, you must go on. You must."

He removed the journal from her hand. He placed it from whence it came. He sported a mischievous grin. "Sly Margaret. Wait until I see her."

"I have an idea." Alyssa was holding him now, whispering in his ear. "Let's drive to Nuthampstead next weekend. We can stay at the Woodman Inn. We'll be able to feel your father. Your mother would be thrilled if we continued reading the journal there." She tugged at his arm, "Please Joseph, please say yes."

"I don't know if I can wait an entire week before reading the next page." He kissed her ear, "But it's a grand idea."

"I'll call to make reservations."

"But my duty schedule. I'm not sure if I'm scheduled for next weekend."

"You're not. I've already checked." She gave him a sensuous grin. Her eyes beckoned. Alyssa extended her hand. She touched Joseph's fingers in an all too familiar way.

"Now," a playful smile crossed his face.

She teased him with her eyes, kissed him passionately, "Yes, dear Joseph, now."

Slowly she unbuttoned his shirt, placed her fingers on his chest.

"Remember what Churchill said, my handsome Captain?"

"And pray tell, my beautiful wife, what did Churchill say?"

Leading him to the unmade bed, she answered, "Well, he said there is a time for words and there is a time for action." Stopping before reaching the bed she smirked, "And this is a time for action."

* * * * *

Several hours later Joseph stared at the ceiling. He casually ran his finger down Alyssa's spine.

"He was a man of wisdom wasn't he?"

"Who," she rolled over to face him.

"Churchill." His mischievous smile turned to laughter.

JOSEPH AND MARGARET HAVE DINNER

OCTOBER 7, 1977
COLTISHALL AIR BASE, ENGLAND

Margaret enjoyed her dinners with young Joseph. In some ways, sitting in the Officers Club at Coltishall, reminded her of years long past. The wartime years, at times, seemed like a distant memory and yet the memories, at moments like these, remained fresh in her mind.

Anne's son was her connection to the days when she was young and vibrant. The days when, despite the horrors of war, she lived each day as it would be her last.

As she relived these youthful times in her mind she was interrupted by a young officer; a quite handsome chap with a disarming grin.

"Excuse me, Miss. You might be Margaret Crueller?"

"Why yes I am," she replied. She studied the features of the young Lieutenant. His youthful face, his wavy hair, and dark brown eyes looked familiar to her.

"Well, Miss. I have a message from Captain Howard. He will be thirty minutes late." He hesitated, not wanting to alarm her. "Just a bit of weather, Miss. Nothing to be concerned with."

Margaret's gaze remained fixed on the young officers face. The officer felt somewhat unsettled.

"Is everything alright, Miss? I mean are you okay?" He seemed a bit nervous.

Margaret realized she was staring at the officer. Then, "Oh, I'm sorry. You just happened to remind me of someone I knew." She paused before continuing, " A long time ago of course." She hesitated and found herself floundering for words. "I'm so sorry. I can't believe how much you look like a gentleman friend of mine." She extended her hand. "Thank you for delivering the message and please Lieutenant forgive me for my intent glare. I'm afraid you have taken me back a few years."

"Oh, no problem, Miss. Happy memories, I'm sure." He paused, nodded, smiled and said, "Cheerio, he'll be along soon, Captain Howard I mean."

She watched as he walked away. He walked like Earl. Second Lieutenant Earl Hart, the young friend of Joseph Doglio. A tear came to her eye. Oh how she wished she could relive those days. She wished that somehow she had the power to change the decision she made so many years ago. The tear slowly made it's way to her lip before resting gently against her face.

"Oh, Earl, you were so . . ."

"I'm sorry Margaret," it was Joseph. "A little weather problem again. We've had our share of it haven't we?"

Looking at her he noticed the tear and the redness in her eyes.

"Margaret, is everything alright? You look distressed." Joseph's voice showed concern.

She stood and held him for what seemed an eternity.

"Everything is fine, Captain. I was just reliving a moment with a fine officer," she faltered, her voice breaking. "I must tell you about him someday. But not tonight." She sat down, "Now young man, what can we talk about this evening. Tell me. I'm eager to listen."

Joseph was reluctant to begin. "Shall we order? Ted tells me the lamb is especially good this evening."

Dinner, for both of them, seemed a bit awkward. Joseph continued to wonder what had made Margaret so emotional. Margaret was taken back by her sudden rush of memories, even more taken back by the thoughts that instantly replayed in her heart.

"Well, young man. You asked me to dinner for a reason. What could it be?"

"Oh, come now Margaret. I don't need a reason to invite you to dinner. What would mum say if I needed a reason to share your company?"

"You officers are so dashing; such a way with words. You haven't changed much through the years. Not the lot of you." She managed a smile and a wink.

Joseph took her hand. "That's better now. The same wicked Margaret that I know." Then laughing he added, "Sly Margaret would be more like it."

"And what on earth does that mean. Wicked I understand, but sly Margaret. Come on now. Explain that to me Captain."

Joseph played with his table service. He knew a few moments of anticipation would arouse dear Margaret's interest.

"Well, enough of your coyness. Let's have it shall we." Her remarks seemed pointed but her smile betrayed her feelings.

"Well Margaret, I read the first entry in my mothers journal."

Suddenly Margaret became serious. She did her best to hide the change in her disposition.

"So you did. And . . ."

"She wrote about her first encounter with my father. It was beautiful Margaret. I can't explain the way it was written. So young, she was, and yet so eager to present herself to father. Do you understand what I'm trying to say?"

"I believe I do. Yes, I recall that first meeting. It was at Rainbow Corner." Margaret seemed to drift back through time.

Joseph explained how he and Alyssa were going to Nuthampstead to read more.

"Is that all you read?" inquired Margaret. "Her first entry?"

Joseph nodded, "Tell me what you remember about that first night. I would like to hear your recollection. I'm so taken with her description of meeting father that I . . ."

Margaret placed her hand on his uniform. "It was June 23, 1944. I remember like it was yesterday."

MARGARET'S RETURN TO LONDON

OCTOBER 7, 1977

The return from Coltishall to London was slightly over an hour. She no longer enjoyed the evening drive. She blamed her disaffection on her age, fifty-five years, and the annoying glare of headlights that seemed to keep her from properly seeing the road.

Joseph, polite as ever, asked her to spend the night at the Air Base but, as usual, she declined, claiming she had morning business in London. Her only business consisted of making her bed and cleaning after her cat, Piccadilly.

She found herself exhausted. It wasn't a physical exhaustion, but a mental exhaustion, as memories of the war years flooded her mind.

Her meandering thoughts seemed to stray from Lieutenant Earl Hart to her concerns about her dear friend's diary. What had Anne written on those pages? What would young Joseph find that might cause him to question his mother's past?

Suddenly, without warning, she felt her tires leave the road. The car began to zigzag and swerve, almost out of control. Margaret struggled with the steering wheel until she finally, after a few harrowing moments, brought the car to a stop.

"Land sakes, what's come over me?" was all she could mutter.

Margaret sat by the side of the road for some time. The engine continued to run. Ahead she noticed a road sign. Perhaps, for the first time in her life, she would find a room and stay the night. Usually the drive from Coltishall to London was uneventful but tonight her mind was not on the road. Her mind and her heart were taken back to war torn London. The year was no longer 1977; the year was 1944.

Finding a room, she sat on the edge of her sofa. She opened a balcony door that was conveniently located next to her bed. The evening breeze brushed across her face reviving more memories and further thoughts of her youth. The plain white draperies that hung from the balcony window seemed to provide a rhythm for her meditation.

The diary. Her thumb rubbed the corner of the bed. The diary. Oh, Anne, what have you written? She recalled the days after Joseph's death, the agonizing days and unending nights of despair. Anne, she thought, would not survive this horrible ordeal. She lost the one person who had suddenly made her young life worth living. At nineteen, Anne was falling apart. Despite her faith, the loss of Joseph left her in a state of depression and total helplessness.

Margaret recalled the concern and misgivings of leaving Anne alone with this overwhelming burden. Margaret believed Anne would surrender to an act of desperation.

And so, she did, but not the act of surrender that troubled Margaret. Anne surrendered to Joseph completely, in a way that would push her to the breaking point. But in time Anne's decision would give her the peace she so richly deserved. Did Anne write about her decision in this aged journal and if so how would young Joseph react? What questions would be asked of her?

* * * * *

Margaret moved to the balcony. The breeze continued to freshen the stillness of the night.

Lieutenant Earl Hart. Yes, she admitted it many times. She was in love with him. Despite her marriage to Phillip, who was fighting somewhere in France, she fell madly in love with this gentle and handsome American.

She and Earl had spent three days together. They did everything under the sun. They laughed at trivial things, visited pub after pub, and they took time to feed the pigeons in Lowdermilk Park. Something her and her husband had never done. It wasn't such a big thing, obviously, but it was the smiles, and the lighthearted feeling that stirred their fondness for each other. They, in some ways, were like the pigeons. Free to come and go as they pleased. And yet, each carried a burden in their heart. Her, a husband, and he a girl back home who eagerly awaited his return. The girl who was wearing his engagement ring!

Margaret recalled the awkward moments. The dancing at Blair Hotel; their bodies so close that every secret craving was unmistakably realized. The long walks to her apartment, with only her torch (flashlight) available to light the ravaged streets of London. They passed through Piccadilly Circle where the Piccadilly commandos turned tricks, openly in the street, for a few schillings.

They were caught, on their second night together, in a dreadful air raid. As hundreds of military personnel and civilians made their way to the underground, they, the two of them, huddled in a doorway. Their arms embraced each other in a way she had never before experienced. Her fear was absorbed by this man who held her tightly in his arms.

She couldn't contain her emotions. She had this craving, this hunger to make love to him. He in turn, she knew, had this same thirst for her.

The last evening spent together started as all others, a walk, a drink at the pub, a stroll through the park, and the usual conversation. She recalled that later, on that last evening, their affection reached a point of no return. The feeling between them was no longer a dalliance but an affection that was venerated by every enchanting feeling between them.

Earl, awkwardly and somewhat clumsily, retained a room at the Blair. They entered the room, embraced each other, and their passion was released. Their emotions and cravings flooded the room. The moment would remain with her for the rest of her days.

They didn't bother to remove the spread that covered the bed instead they gently lowered themselves onto the flowered covering.

Then, as quickly as the evening had begun, it ended. Perhaps it was because they had a love for each other that went beyond the boundaries. But it was those very boundaries that would not allow them to pursue their passions.

Margaret cried. She cried hysterically. She said she was sorry. Earl stroked her hair and said he understood. They walked through the rubble until they reached her apartment. His arms were strong, full of strength; he hugged her for the last time.

"I'll miss you," he whispered.

"Oh, Earl. And I you! Please believe me will you. I'm madly in love with you." She wiped her tears. "You know that don't you?"

"Only too well; only too well."

Kissing his cheek she went on, "You will come by with Joseph from time to time? Promise you will?"

He shook his head, "You know I will. If you need something, let Anne know. She'll get word to Joseph."

"Earl. . ." he placed his finger on her lips.

"Bye, sweets. Be safe."

Earl turned to walk away. He took several steps. Margaret ran after him.

"I can't say goodbye. Earl, I can't."

They embraced again. The minutes passed. "Off with you now," he said. With this final goodbye Earl disappeared into the shadows. Margaret stood alone. The sound of his footsteps had fallen victim to the darkness of the night.

A gust of wind broke Margaret's reverie. She was aware of the moistness on her face.

Then, almost as she had done some thirty-three years earlier, her emotions could not be restrained.

She shouted into the night. "Oh, Earl, I'm sorry. I'm so sorry." She cried into the morning hours. She felt his presence. Her only wish was that somehow he had forgiven her.

* * * * *

Margaret's husband, Private First Class Francis Phillip Crueller, was killed on December 18, 1944. He lost his life while storming a German bunker.

MARGARET'S REVELATION

7 OCTOBER, 1977
HOTEL ROOM

Margaret's ruminations about the journal took her back in time to Anne's last painful days. So much morphine was being pumped into her cancer-ravaged body, that most of the time Margaret kept a silent vigil over her dear friend's deathbed. Thus, it was nothing less than miraculous when, during the last week of her life, Anne suddenly regained enough lucidity to speak with Margaret about her last wishes. Only then did Margaret become aware that her friend had been keeping an intimate journal for all those years. Margaret remembered the tear that slowly slid down Anne's cheek as she struggled to express her concern that Joseph Earl have the journal. It was the story of his life, as well as hers. Margaret immediately understood that Anne had invested everything in this journal, planning for the day it would be placed in her son's hands. It was her lifeline, and had been all along.

Margaret held Anne's fragile hand as she promised to deliver the journal to Joseph. But Anne had one last favor to ask of her: "Write my last entry for me." Reaching for the worn leather-bound book, Margaret realized this was to be her friend's last struggle, her swan song. She was thinking of how fleeting life is when Anne's strained voice began to whisper, "Everything I've done has been out of my undying love for Lieutenant Joseph Doglio, my Joey." Anne spoke so slowly that Margaret had no trouble getting each word down verbatim.

> *Everything I've done has been out of my undying love for Lieutenant Joseph Doglio, my Joey. Often I've wondered how different my life might have been had we never been fortunate enough to have met. If given a chance I'd gladly relive all those moments again, and I'd make all the same choices. We kept our promise to each other, you and I. Even in my darkest hour, I've felt your gentle, unwavering support. Surely few can attest to sharing what we two shared. As I lie here drawing my last breath, I know you await me on the other side. Oh, what a joyous reunion this promises to be! I leave behind a son who has given me the most splendid joys life has to offer.*

You have been a true blessing to me, my dearest. Now that you have learned the firsthand account of our story, I pray you have become enriched by the beauty of its meaning. I've always tried to do what's right for you; now you must follow that which rings true in your heart. Know that your father and I will never be too far away. Be brave, my son; it is your birthright. I cannot put into words how much I love you. . . .

Silence reclaimed the atmosphere in the hospital room, save for the ticking of the clock on the night stand next to Anne's bed. Margaret looked up from the journal to see a look of sheer reverie upon Anne's face. She almost appeared to be smiling. Her eyes were now shut, and the same tear she had shed earlier remained glistening inextricably upon her cheek. "Anne, just how thorough have you been with your journal here?" Margaret hinted softly. But Anne made no reply. She had summoned the strength to surface one last time from the murky depths of morphine to deliver this, her last message. Peace enveloped her two days later.

* * * * *

Margaret splashed the cool tap water onto her face as she recalled the feeling of uncertainty left with her after recording Anne's last entry. She was experiencing that same feeling tonight. Her mind began drifting back further in time to the night of Anne's twentieth birthday. Margaret had organized a little get-together at her flat in hopes of raising Anne's spirits. Joseph's death had really taken its toll on her friend, having virtually sealed herself up in her room since receiving the devastating news. So Margaret thought a little social interface might be just what Anne needed to lift her out of this funk. "She needs to move on," Margaret murmured to herself as she changed into her nightgown. But she needed a nudge, she did. Only something had happened that night which would change the course of Anne's life forever; something known only to two other people besides Anne and Margaret. "And perhaps that bloody journal," Margaret worried. . . .

* * * * *

The weather had been dreary for weeks in London, but the rain was really coming down the evening of Anne's twentieth birthday. It was the third of September, 1944. Margaret silently cursed the elements as she bustled about her flat, putting things just so for the evening's festivities. "It's a wonder we've not all lost our minds, between this dreadful weather and a never-ending war," she mused. She was especially concerned for Anne: she knew how attached she'd grown to Joseph, but Margaret had reckoned her friend would be strong enough to put the loss into perspective. It has been weeks since they learned the news of the *Angel* crew, and Anne wasn't coping well. If anything, she appeared to be slipping away with each passing day.

Her parents were worried sick about her, and, frankly, so was Margaret. Her days volunteering at the Admiralty had not ceased, but she had lost her enthusiasm. And when she was home she shut herself up in that room of hers, refusing even to eat. "Come on, gal, you've got to make it over this!" Margaret had finally pleaded with her. "Don't you think I miss Earl? Don't you think I cry myself to sleep at night, thinking of what could have been? Those boys died the most noble death imaginable. Generations will honor them. Can't you see that their deaths had the greatest purpose of all? You might try feeling some pride in having known Joseph for the short time that you did. That alone ought to give you strength. Please try to remember that he didn't come all the way to Europe to meet and fall in love with you, my dear. He came to fight a war for our freedom. I don't mean to sound so blunt, but you've got to get a grip on the situation. You have to accept what has happened and move on. . ."

Perhaps those words had penetrated Anne's psyche, because she finally agreed that being in the company of friends might do her some good. Margaret was thrilled to arrange it all. She wanted the atmosphere to be festive, but intimate and supportive. She had invited only a dozen or so people, and planned to have the entirety of her small flat lit only by candles. She knew how much Anne loved the candlelight.

Margaret had taken the liberty of inviting Charles Spencer, though she hadn't informed Anne of this. Foppish as he no doubt was, he could be quite entertaining in a social context; and Margaret was willing to put up with him for an evening if he could provide some amusing distraction for Anne. "I hope I don't live to regret this," Margaret had thought, when, predictably, Charles was the first guest to arrive that evening. "Hullo, Maggie. I thought I'd bring these roses for Anne. As I recall, she loves the color burgundy."

"Wonderful," Margaret speculated as she took his overcoat, "something else to remind her of Joseph. I hate it when he calls me Maggie. . ."

When Anne arrived, Margaret was there to meet her at the door. She had walked the short distance from her parents house in the rain, and wore an expression that almost looked as if she were lost. Her hair and the little bit of make-up she wore looked off-kilter, as if she'd attempted to paint on a happy face to conceal the misery she felt inside. Margaret locked her in an embrace. "Please try to put your troubles aside and enjoy yourself tonight," Margaret whispered encouragingly in her ear.

Anne did do her best to appear gracious, but the strain was evident to everyone gathered at Margaret's that evening. The hollowness of each word she spoke, coupled with the vacant look in her eyes, almost made her seem an imposter for the real Anne Howard. The other guests made every effort to be discreet in their concern for her, but the entire evening was marred with awkwardness. Even the usual antics of Charles Spencer were slightly subdued. He was, however, perhaps the one person who enjoyed himself that evening; his main objective always being to have a good time.

Charles knew of the loss Anne had suffered. He was the only person in the room besides Margaret who had actually met Joseph – that night at Covent Gardens. Yet Charles was so accustomed to attracting the attentions of young ladies, that his constant attempts at flirtation with Anne were beginning to present a challenge to his ego. Anne, you see, couldn't have been more despondent. In his characteristically jaded manner, he conveniently placed Anne's suffering secondary to his own childish need for female conquest. By evening's end he had managed to ask Anne if he could give her a lift home no less than a half-dozen times, and each time she declined. Oddly enough, though, he had somehow made his mark.

Charles lingered on with Anne and Margaret after the other guests had left. The weather had not improved, but Anne still insisted on walking. "It's not that far, Margaret, and I have my umbrella. I'll be fine, really," she had said, as the two embraced by the front door. And though the evening's overall atmosphere hadn't been as uplifting as Margaret had hoped, Anne did actually seem to be a bit less remote in attitude. The two kissed one another on the cheek, and Anne disappeared down the front steps.

Margaret warily returned to the living room, where she imagined Charles would likely try to make his advances with her, having had no luck with Anne. But to her pleasant surprise, Charles was gathering his overcoat and bidding her goodnight. "It's been fun, love," he said sarcastically. as she walked him to the door. "I hope Anne snaps out of it soon.

She's too fine a woman to risk ending up a spinster." The door was open for him to leave, but to the surprise of both, they saw Anne across the street, talking under the old bakery awning with what appeared to be a Yank.

Charles was the first to call out, "Anne, is that Yank bothering you?" She cast a quick glance their way and immediately returned her attention to the unknown man.

"Anne, do you need to come back inside?" Margaret's voice projected across the darkened street. Charles began making his way down the front steps in their direction. At the same moment, Anne and the stranger were crossing the street to Margaret's. Anne had her hand on the man's elbow. She introduced him as Sergeant Mark Dixon, a friend of Joseph's. She practically begged him to come inside, but he said he really must be off. Anne and this Dixon shook hands, and she stood there staring after him in the rain with the most curious expression on her face.

After some time, she turned to Margaret, "Do you mind if I have a bit of private time back inside?" Charles followed the two women indoors, even though he had not been invited.

When Margaret took Anne's coat again, she noticed an envelope pushed down the front of her blouse. "He brought me a letter from Joey," Anne said in a faraway voice. She drifted down the hall and shut herself in Margaret's room. Margaret continued to stand there by the front door, pondering this sudden twist of events. She then became irritated when she realized Charles had again made himself comfortable in the living room.

"This has nothing to do with that pest," she mumbled under her breath as she turned to go ask him to leave. She had just about managed to get rid of him, when the door to Margaret's room opened. Anne emerged with an inexplicable look of beatitude upon her face. She was smiling.

"I think I'll take you up on that offer for a ride home now, Charles. If you don't mind. . ." She then turned to Margaret, kissed her on the cheek, and whispered, "I'll ring you tomorrow. Thank you for persuading me to come out tonight."

* * * * *

In the plush interior of Charles Spencer's car, Anne took a detour home that night. Though her course of action was unorthodox, it was the first thing that made sense to her fragile state-of-mind since the day she learned of Joseph's death.

* * * * *

The birth certificate relating to young Joseph's birth was changed. The actual records forever removed by an influential father who would do anything to protect his family name and the name of his wayward son.

* * * * *

During the years that followed Anne began each day with a prayer. Each day she asked for God's mercy and God's forgiveness.

* * * * *

From the day her son was born, Anne believed, in her mind, and in her heart, that Joseph, her handsome and her beloved Second Lieutenant was the boy's father. She kept her promise to give Joseph the son both he and she had dreamed of.

* * * * *

When the doctor placed her newborn son in her arms Margaret overheard Anne whisper to her son, "I kept my promise, Joseph. We have our son."

MARK DIXON

1977
BEAUFORT, SOUTH CAROLINA, USA

Years of hard work had taken a toll on Mark Dixon. Since his return from his duties as a crew chief for the 398th Bomb Group in Nuthampstead, England, in 1945, he had not missed one day of work. He was a graying fifty-seven year old man, a widower, who had built a successful business and an honest reputation serving Beaufort as a mechanic and the proud owner of a modest service station.

His current customers were the same customers who frequented his business in 1947. Now their children stopped by for a fill up and whatever mechanical work that needed to be done on modern automobiles that seemed to need less and less attention.

Mark Dixon's once dark black hair had streaks of gray, not just around the temples, but everywhere. The crevices on his hands had acquired years of residue produced by oil spills and the spray of dark brown grease, gone astray, from a hand held grease gun. At fifty-seven, he was losing the use of his thumbs; one finger had been broken, but not reset, as he stubbornly refused to see a doctor. His stubbornness left his left index finger frozen in an immovable position, the first joint left to dangle in a downward projection.

Even his eyes, ever weakening, strained with his store bought glasses. Once again he refused to take the time to visit the eye doctor who just happened to have an office across the street from his service station.

The aging man lived on the outskirts of town. His well maintained home sat on the edge of the marshlands in the low country of Beaufort County. An occasional alligator would take refuge under his one hundred year old oak tree. His dog. Pal, an aging golden retriever, served as the unofficial greeter for all unsuspected guests, but now, after years of customary visits, the dark green alligator was, to him, a member of the family. Pal no longer barked a warning of *Old Pete's* arrival.

Dixon had one daughter. She was, in his mind, the finest daughter a father could wish for. She gave him a granddaughter and now, after several years of teaching, she spent time looking after him. In many ways, she, along with her husband, took care of all the little things his wife had done for so many years.

Besides all the living gifts God had given him he prized two photographs. Two aged and fading photos; one of a World War II aircrew, and the other of a Second Lieutenant and a beautiful young woman. The photo of the aircrew hung on the wall behind the cash register at his service station. The other was placed on the cluttered bookshelf in his home, next to a cross bearing the body of his Lord.

People in Beaufort were familiar with the photograph of the crew. Customers often asked Mark to tell them about the crew. Now, new customers, or just plain folks passing through asked him the same question.

"Were you a member of the crew?"

"No," he answered.

"Then who are they," the customers would ask.

"The *Angel* crew," he responded, kindly. "They met their maker on July 19, 1944." "I," he proudly proclaimed, "was their crew chief."

"Oh," and then, to his dismay, no further questions were asked.

Except once, by his daughter and a local minister who happened to be present on the day he hung the picture, May 2, 1947.

His reply was the only time he talked about the crew. It seemed that now, thirty-two years after the war, people were curious, but not so curious to want to know the mysteries of this special World War II crew.

* * * * *

First there was the B-17 itself. A fortress that glowed in the morning sun. Not the usual glow, but something that seemed to radiate across the entire airbase. The glow was strange and even spiritual. Dixon noticed the difference the first time he worked on *Angel.* Her long fuselage and four Wright Cyclone Engines seemed to give him a sublime feeling. To compound his feelings he found the crew to be deeply religious. All except the tail gunner, who by some miracle, after the war, became a Brother for a Franciscan Monastery in Italy.

During one of his many lengthy repairs of *Angel* he was taken back by the religious messages that were taped near the positions of crew members.

Angel, at times appeared to talk to him. Preparing him for what was to come.

Dixon witnessed the tear under the angel's eye. A tear, he knew, that was not painted by a human hand.

He was taken by Carroll O'Neill's sudden appearance on July 19, 1944, the day of *Angel's* last flight; Carroll O'Neill who rushed from the darkness of the early morning shadows of Base 131 to tell his crew mates that he "wished them Godspeed." Those words, coming from O'Neill, were spooky, almost ominous.

On July 19, 1944, Second Lieutenant Dallas Hawkins told him, *"He had been a good friend."* "Had been," was the way he said it.

Of course there were the stories that filtered down to him from other members of the 398th. Stories of Earl Hart's play book and how it suddenly appeared to Earl's mother some four years after his death.

There was the mystery of the window in Doglio's bedroom. On the day of his burial it was opened eight inches. The same as it had been during his boyhood years in South Wilmington, Illinois. Who opened it, who placed the plywood shield in place and how could anyone have done it considering Second Lieutenant Doglio's room had been locked for five years. Mrs. Doglio demanded the room be forever closed until Joseph, her son, returned home.

And there was the unexplainable return of the gold locket that Anne Howard had given Doglio just days before his final mission. Dixon himself had given the locket to the base commander and asked that it be sent home with Joseph's effects.

How then in July of 1955 did someone, apparently dressed in a Second Lieutenant uniform from World War II, return the locket to Miss Howard?

Since those war years he swore there were times when he felt the presence of the angel crew. One day, he himself was taken by a mysterious circumstance that took place at his service station. This curious and puzzling event continued to be a defining moment in his spiritual life and the event forever strengthened his religious beliefs.

In 1964, two days before Thanksgiving, he finished his work on Mr. Zanello's pick up truck. The hour was late, past closing time. Wiping his hands of oil, he turned the lights off in the garage and made his way into his office. He called it an office, but in reality, it was where his customers would sit while waiting for their car.

On the wood and glass counter was his cash register and behind the register, on the wall, was the photograph of the angel crew. On this late evening he was startled as he approached the office. He saw a figure move toward the counter. He became alarmed, as he had earlier locked the doors. The hour was late and the streets of Beaufort were void of people.

Only the corner streetlight gave proof of the earlier activity on the road passing his business.

He moved closer, quietly, until he saw a man staring at the photograph. The man didn't move. He just seemed to stare at the faces of the nine-man crew.

Opening the door to the office Dixon offered his usual greeting. He tried to greet the stranger in his usual calm voice but his instincts told him something was unnatural about this scene before him.

"Can I help you?" he offered in a slow southern accent.

The stranger turned to face him. A gentle smile crossed the face of his visitor. "You already have," the stranger moved to the door, turned and offered, "Thank you Sergeant, ummmmm, Mr. Dixon.'

With that he was gone.

Dixon seemed frozen, staring through the plate glass window. He watched as the man disappeared into the night. Shaken by what he thought was a familiarity in the way the man walked and by the smile that seemed to be so familiar he reached to check the lock on the door. Strange he thought. It was locked. How did the stranger get in, how did he leave? The key to the door was in his cash register.

Shaking his head in disbelief, Dixon returned to the counter.

"My God," he uttered. A chill came over him.

Lying on the counter was a familiar Saint Christopher medal. He couldn't bring himself to touch it. He stared in amazement at the religious token and then collecting his emotions he knelt on the dust-laden floor and gave thanks that his belief in miracles had been confirmed.

* * * * *

There were three hallmarks of Dixon's character. Three undeniable attributes of this humble mechanic that the people of Beaufort, South Carolina knew for a fact: First, he was a good father; second, he was a spiritual man, a man with deep-rooted religious beliefs. Perhaps a result of what he had seen during the war years. And third, he was as honest and sincere as the day was long.

If ever there was a saint in Beaufort it was he, Mark Dixon.

CAPTAIN JOSEPH HOWARD

DECEMBER 18, 1977
OFF THE ENGLISH COAST
NEAR COLTISHALL

Joseph and his friend, Captain Todd Early were engaged in a training mission, a dogfight over the Atlantic Ocean. Each pilot, several times a week, would do battle with fellow officers. Joseph looked forward to his duels with Captain Early. Both Early and he were considered to be the finest pilots in the Jaguar Air Group.

Joseph enjoyed doing battle with Todd, not only because of his remarkable skills, but because, as friends, the winner enjoyed bragging rights as well as the opportunity to receive a winners dinner at the Officers Club.

Joseph's Jaguar, *Angel*, broke away from Todd. Banking hard to his left, Joseph radioed his friend.

"Next time you see me, old friend, I'll be on your tail." Then as usual he added his now celebrated line, "I am the

Angel of death. I came from the skies. Unannounced. Prepare to meet your maker."

Todd watched Joseph's Jaguar disappear from sight. He climbed to 30,000 feet before entering a bank of clouds. Joseph had disappeared from his radar screen.

Angel was heading due north at speeds in excess of seven hundred fifty miles per hour. Joseph altered his course to west, southwest. The Jaguar made a wide swing until the sun was at his six. Then, silently, Joseph maneuvered *Angel* toward Todd.

"There he is!" a blip showed on his screen. He pressed the throttle forward; the force pressed him against the pilot seat. The Saint Christopher medal reflected in the sunlight. "I'm on his screen now," Joseph said out loud. "Too late friend. You're all mine."

Breaking through the clouds, Todd was directly below him. *Angel's* air speed approached eight hundred twenty-five miles per hour. The miles closed quickly.

Todd calculated Joseph's attack to take place in forty-two seconds. At thirty-nine seconds Todd throttled his Jaguar to a higher speed and then turned upward, toward the blue skies.

Angel reacted immediately. Pursuing her pray, *Angel* forced herself to the limit. She would not allow *Pepito,* Todd's aircraft, to out maneuver her.

Joseph smiled as he refused to be shaken from Todd's tail. Then, unexpectedly, Todd reduced his airspeed, dramatically, coming dangerously close to stalling his Jaguar.

Joseph couldn't react in time. *Angel* raced past *Pepito* as if he was standing still.

"I'll be damned," Joseph muttered.

Now he was the hunted.

Todd powered his Jaguar and in seconds he was on Joseph's tail.

"Who's the angel of death now my friend?"

Joseph banked again and then again. The sonic booms could be heard for miles. The pilots maneuvered their Jaguars with incredible skill. Todd came closer, ready to claim his kill, but not to be outdone; Joseph rolled his *Angel* and then looped into a tight circle that would have caused most pilots to lose consciousness.

Todd, in *Pepito*, hurled forward and then turned 360 degrees for a frontal attack on *Angel.*

The radar screens on both *Angel* and *Pepito* showed they were on a collision course. Closer, ever closer, at speeds reserved for mortal combat.

Suddenly, they were in eye contact. Who would blink first? Each spec became lager until Todd swore he could see Joseph eyes.

"Christ." Todd yelled.

Pepito banked left and *Angel* banked to her left. Their wingtips seemed to scrape together as the sudden veer caused the wind to scream against the fuselage of both Jaguars.

Neither pilot spoke. Todd was shaking. In all his flying days he had not encountered a dogfight such as this.

"You there, *Pepito*?"

"You're a bloody crazy man!" came the reply.

Angel appeared on his wingtip.

Joseph ventured, "A draw, what do you think?"

Todd held his reply for a moment. "I'll let you know when I remove my pants."

Both pilots sped through the sky. *Angel* and *Pepito* glistened in the sunlight.

Joseph broke the silence, "Let's go home!"

"Good by me. Who buys?"

"Won't know until you inspect your underwear."

Todd grinned, gave Joseph the thumbs up. Coltishall was one hour away.

* * * * *

Captain Todd Early was the same age as Joseph. While Joseph had come from a humble background, Todd was the son of Lord Early, a renowned British Member of Parliament.

They had few things in common when it came to their backgrounds, but in the air they were equals, more than that they were the best of friends. They protected each other no matter what the circumstances.

* * * * *

The friendship would have a dramatic and lasting effect on their lives. For one, the friendship would bring an end to his life.

HOLIDAY DINNER
JOSEPH, ALYSSA, TODD, DENISE

DECEMBER 23, 1977
COLTISHALL AIRBASE

The couples enjoyed the holiday dinner. The festive occasion had become a tradition. A tradition that began four years ago. The friendship between two Royal Air Force Captains had been cultivated through the years.

Alyssa often found their relationship to be a little bizarre. Todd, a product of a well established British family, and her husband, Joseph, the son of a modest woman. A woman who found life to be such a challenge.

Alyssa was well aware that the success of her husband, in many ways, could be attributed to the manner in which he was raised. Anne found time from her duties at the Admiralty to give Joseph the love and guidance he so desperately needed.

Joseph, during his childhood years, was a high-strung young man. He was full of energy. Some said he didn't recognize the meaning of fear. Joseph was constantly exploring, testing himself, and his mother, to the limits.

Anne, with her absolute patience, kept her wits about her. She allowed young Joseph to test the limits of life.

Todd, on the other hand, was raised on an 1100-acre estate. His father was a noted Member of Parliament. His mother was a member of British society. Both parents had received audiences with the queen.

By the time Todd was eleven he was an expert horseman. Social graces were a defining part of his upbringing.

At the age of twelve, Todd was picking flowers from the exquisite gardens that surrounded "Hadley House", the proper name for his family estate.

As Todd picked flowers, Joseph was picking his nose, nursing cuts and bruises, and taking time along life's journey to learn about his father, a navigator, in the American 398th Bomb Group. The father he never knew, the father he wished he had, had become an obsession to him. He hungered for knowledge of this father of his, Second Lieutenant Joseph Doglio.

Despite the differences in their social training, Joseph and Todd had one similarity. They both had a craving to fly. For Joseph, it was an itch. An itch that ate at his very soul.

He wanted to own the skies as his father had owned them during World War II.

As Joseph grew older he knew the blood of his father was stirring inside him. Secretly he saved every penny from delivering newspapers and performing odd jobs. Finally, at the age of fourteen, he convinced a Mr. Fellows to give him flying lessons. Reluctantly Mr. Fellows took young Joseph into the air and from that moment on, Joseph became the owner of the skies his father had once cherished.

At the age of seventeen Joseph was flying solo in a way that caused experienced pilots to take second looks.

Meanwhile, Todd was intrigued with the aircraft of the Royal Air Force. His father gained entrance to the air bases across England. Todd was soon privileged to discuss the art of flying with some of the finest pilots in England.

As fate would have it, their paths crossed, as both Joseph and Todd entered the Royal Air Force. The date was February 5, 1965.

From that day on they became inseparable; each learning from the other. Todd, so to speak, was learning to pick his nose, and Joseph was learning the finer qualities of life. In time they became unrelated brothers.

Joseph visited “Hadley House” on many occasions. He learned to ride, to hunt,

and from trial and error, he humorously learned to speak to a Member of Parliament.

Todd, on the other hand, enjoyed visits to Anne’s humble home. She taught him how to make a mince pie, how to laugh at the smallest things in life, and most importantly, how to give of oneself. In his short life, Todd had not seen such a devoted and caring person. She loved her son, Todd knew, beyond all reasonable limits.

He also noticed the evidence of her husband, an American Lieutenant, was everywhere.

Todd asked Anne to tell him about this handsome Second Lieutenant. Anne smiled and meekly said, “He was my knight in shining armor.” Her voice wavered. “There will never be another like him.”

With that she wiped her hands on her plain white apron and slowly walked from the room.

Todd walked to the sideboard located against the far wall. There he admired a photograph of young Joseph’s father. Handsome, he thought. Alongside the photo was another, this containing an entire crew standing before a B-17 Flying Fortress with an angel proudly painted on the forward fuselage. On the corner of the sideboard was a silver frame, 8x10 in size. A young Lieutenant, handsome but looking somewhat shy, held his arm around an attractive and very beautiful young woman. The woman wore the uniform of an Admiralty volunteer. Joseph's father and mother, he thought.

"They made a most handsome couple, didn't they?" Joseph joined him.

"Your mother and father?" Todd pointed curiously at the photograph.

"Yes," Joseph took the photograph in his hands. "He was a fine man, mom says," he paused. "Well, she must tell you someday."

Truth was that as much as he knew about his father, there was much he didn't know. There was much he wanted to know

* * * * *

"Well, another year." Denise broke the silence.

"Sorry," Joseph apologized. "I'm a little out of sorts, aren't I?" He half smiled at Alyssa.

"It's all right, old man," Todd nodded. "It's perfectly understandable."

Alyssa seized the moment. "I know it may not be the time, but Joseph, why not share some of the incredible discoveries you found in mom's diary."

Her words seemed to hang in the air. She hoped Joseph would seize them and break his sullen mood. His first holiday, absent his mother's presence, seemed to distress him more than she realized.

"Incredible! That sounds rather intriguing. Pray tell, what have you found." Todd seized the words from Alyssa and did his best to move the moment along.

"Well, yes. I guess you might say intriguing. Rather mysterious revelations." Joseph spoke in a low whisper, his voice almost distant.

Silence, once again, settled around the table.

Denise placed her hand on Joseph's wrist. "Maybe we can discuss this next time. Perhaps. . ."

"No, no. It's perfectly alright." Joseph smiled apologetically. "Sorry. I've been somewhat of a dreadful bore, haven't I?"

"Well, once again, where do I begin?"

Several hours later Joseph finished telling them about the tear under angels eye. The spiritual nature of the crew and of his fathers remains being returned to the US. He spent time telling them about the window in his father's room, how it was cracked open, eight-inches the night of his funeral.

He told of the play book found by Second Lieutenant Earl Hart's parents.

The most intriguing story was how the locket, given to his father by his mother in 1944, was returned mysteriously to his mother in 1955 while she prayed at Saint Georges Church in Anstey, England.

Todd and Denise were captivated by the stories. They were taken by the strange events. So much so that they asked question after question.

One question asked by Todd, "How did you learn of these incredible events?"

Joseph was alive now. Excited that he had shared the stories with his friends.

"In mom's journal I found a rather long letter from a chap named Mark Dixon. Seems he was the crew chief for *Angel*, my father's Fortress.

"And. . ." Denise queried, her voice aroused with curiosity.

"And this Dixon chap wrote mom, some time ago, about the puzzling events that followed the families of the crew and also about his own personal feelings regarding the *Angel* crew. It's an extraordinary letter."

The conversation continued. Alyssa, although not voicing her opinion to Joseph, was skeptical of the stories. She believed them to be mysterious, sure, but certainly strange. Yes, even outlandish.

If they were indeed true, there was surely an explanation for the events detailed in Dixon's letter. She chose to keep her opinions to herself, fearing Joseph would not continue with the reading of Anne's beautiful journal. At the proper time, she would voice an opinion about the mysteries.

* * * * *

Joseph added a final story. The story of an event that took place in May of 1975.

"Do you remember the day I had an engine flame out over the North Sea?" He told the story of his Saint Christopher medal and how his *Angel* came to life just seconds before plunging into the sea and taking his life.

"Even more strange," he continued, 'was that when I gained control of my actions, *Angel* was on a direct course for Coltishall.'

"What do you make of it?" was Denise's reply.

"I can only assume," Joseph hesitated for a moment. "I can only assume that some Devine hand pulled *Angel* out of her dive and then set my Jaguar on a direct course for home."

"Do you really believe that?" Todd asked in a sincere way.

"Yes, I do. I believe it was my father's way of telling me he is with me. That he once took his *Angel* home across the North Sea and he, I believe, was telling me that . . ." Alyssa interrupted, "Well, now you know the story. Amazing isn't it?"

They exchanged gifts before Todd and Denise left for "Hadley House."

"Have a great holiday," Todd embraced Alyssa. He and Joseph shook hands, a strong and reassuring clasp of hands.

Alyssa and Denise made plans to meet after the first of the year. Both Joseph and Alyssa saw Todd and Denise to their car and then they were alone. Christmas was two days away.

* * * * *

Alyssa's flowing blonde hair seemed to vary in length. On a windy day it flowed in the wind, blowing across her shoulders in a wispy manner. On a calm day it seemed short, neatly in place. Every strand of blonde hair exactly where it should be. Her blue eyes were the perfect companion for her hair as well as her complexion. Joseph, years earlier, was attracted to her natural beauty and, as he playfully told her, her unwavering knowledge of all things, both large and small.

Alyssa's father was a veterinarian. Through his understanding of life, she found her fondness for animals to grow with each passing day. As a child, she cherished every moment spent at her father's modest animal hospital. She fed the puppies, and she stroked the fur of the playful kittens. When the occasion presented itself, she would follow her father to "Spring Mountain Farm" to tend the Arabian horses belonging to Mr. Watson. During those visits, her father magically produced a lump of sugar or several bright orange carrots that she eagerly fed to the nearest colt that frolicked in the well-maintained green pastures of "Spring Mountain."

Becky, her mother, raised Alyssa and her sisters with a mother's loving care. She nurtured the girls in every conceivable way. From social graces to academics, no stone was left unturned.

Her father suspected Alyssa would follow his footsteps and enter the field of veterinary medicine, but she surprised him and indicated she wanted to become a barrister. Somewhat taken back by her choice, he smiled and accepted her decision.

"Who knows, Alyssa, I may need your expertise someday."

"Heavens, father, what on earth for?" she chided. "You haven't lost a patient yet."

It was her legal training that caused her to doubt the aged letter from that chap, Dixon. Being a barrister, she trusted the facts and to her, facts were stories that could be verified. Verified beyond a reasonable doubt.

Dixon's letter was intriguing but somewhat vague, as he offered no eyewitness accounts or documents containing a verification of his wild tales.

Yes, she admitted, Anne swore the story of the locket's return was true. Even the stately vicar of the church had verified her account of the day's events, July 19, 1955.

But even she could find a possible explanation for the incident. Then again, her explanation was a fabrication of an imaginary theory that she herself had developed in her mind. Her story, she admitted, was based on theory and not hard facts.

Dixon, she thought, was the key. Could she find him? Where did he live? For that matter, was he still alive? She made it her goal to find him, to talk to him and learn more about the mysteries and spiritual encounters of her husband's father and crew. She, by nature, was enthralled with the merits of a legal case, and this matter was one that had tremendous family implications.

If Joseph wanted to believe the stories, she could understand his reasons. For her, however, she must look for the truth, whatever that truth may be.

The key was Staff Sergeant Mark Dixon, the crew chief of a World War II B-17 Flying Fortress named, *Angel.*

Alyssa would begin her search in the morning.

THE GIFT

JANUARY 16, 1978
LONDON, ENGLAND

The doctor told her there was no mistake. Alyssa was pregnant. The due date was September 1st. She could hardly contain her excitement. She must tell Joseph. Then she thought better of it. She would make it special, perhaps an evening in London, at a fancy hotel, with all the romantic trappings of a steamy night of passion.

She giggled at the thought. Dancing, perhaps a stroll across the veranda and then an unforgettable night in each other's arms. In the morning, with the rising of the sun she would tell him the news.

Alyssa, on her return home, stopped at the lingerie shop. She purchased an alluring and seductive negligee. It was white, with long slits from the ankle to the waist. When she walked, her long and beautiful legs were seductively visible. The top portion of the gown was finished in a see through lace that completely exposed her breasts.

It was perfect and this was something she had not done for several years. Joseph, she smiled, would love it. No, more than that, he would be seduced by it. Her smile turned to a naughty grin.

* * * * *

Joseph, having completed another AAR exercise, returned home at half past seven that evening. To his surprise, he found a note on the dinning table. It was addressed to him.

My dearest Captain:

I have been summoned to London. Some barrister work I'm afraid. Sorry for not getting word to you. It all came up so suddenly. I checked with Sergeant Shipley. He told me you were not on duty this weekend.

I took the liberty of making a Friday evening reservation at the Savoy.
Hurry will you! I can't wait to see you, alone. Need I say more?

Alys

He shook his head. The Savoy. My god! I hope the barrister wages will pay for the evening. Then, he sat back and pictured an evening with his wife, away from the shrill noise of jet engines and military Jaguars.

"And no, my dear cajoling wife, there is no need to say more," he said to himself. He couldn't contain his excitement.

* * * * *

The dinner was excellent. Roast duck with an orange sauce that covered both duck and potatoes. There was a side of dark green asparagus and a piece of key lime pie for dessert.

"Don't eat too much dessert, handsome flyer. The best dessert is yet to come." Alyssa looked him in the eye. Her eyes captivated him with a naughty twinkle.

"I have often heard it said that two desserts are better than one," he teased.

"Well, that may be true, my dear, but tonight I'm all the dessert you can handle," she teased him with her eyes and her lips.

"Why don't we get the check?" he stammered.

"So far, that is the best suggestion you've had all night." Then she added, "But then again, the night has only just begun."

* * * * *

The Savoy suite was beautiful. A large sitting area decorated with large wood pieces, a light brown carpet with ceiling to floor draperies adding just the right touch of color. The room had several pictures; one, a colorful depiction of a garden party with joyful guests enjoying the fruits of the days harvest.

The bedroom was large and yet tastefully decorated. There was a king size bed covered with a rich and very thick white comforter. The draperies matched the bed covering thus adding a continuous flow to the decor.

The carpet was thick and lush enticing one to feel the full cushion of comfort under one's feet. Soft enough to lie on, Alyssa thought.

Over the bed was a picture of a maiden, breasts exposed, carrying a flower basket to some unknown destination. The maiden had a playful and mischievous smile on her face.

It was all so perfect, Alyssa thought.

She unbuckled his belt and moved her hand across his chest. "Why don't you get comfortable? I'll join you in a minute."

The bed was soft, just as he liked it. His anticipation was getting the best of him. Alyssa knew it would, so she made him wait a few extra minutes.

Opening the bedroom door, she stood in the glow of the light. Her body was outlined by the light in such a way that her breasts were visible through the laced top of her negligee. As she walked toward him the long slits of her gown exposed her shapely legs to Joseph's waiting eyes.

"And which part of dessert would you like first, my dear?" Then she added, "Your choice."

He studied her, admiring her beauty. How had he been so lucky to find and marry someone so beautiful, so loving, and so committed to making him the happiest man in the world.

He gently took her hand and lowered her body to the bed. "I think I'll begin here," he touched her breasts and kissed her softly.

* * * * *

He awoke to a knock on the door.

"What on earth," it was six-thirty a.m.

"Alyssa," he seemed confused. Alyssa was not in bed. He began to get up but he heard Alyssa's voice as she talked to someone at the door.

"Oh, no!" he thought aloud. "Something has happened at the base."

"Thank you," Alyssa could be heard through the opened bedroom door.

She returned to the bedroom, but before entering she instructed Joseph to close his eyes.

"What's this all about?" he questioned. "What on earth is going on?"

"Close your eyes," she teasingly demanded.

Alyssa walked through the door. She pushed a baby stroller that had been stored at the registration desk. Inside the stroller was an envelope. The envelope simply said, "I love you."

Stopping beside the bed, she whispered in his ear. "I have a surprise for my Captain. But you can't open your eyes until you promise you'll reward me by repeating last night's performance."

"That, my dear sweetie, will be a pleasure."

"For you then."

He opened his eyes. Joseph was speechless. A tear came to his eye. She brushed at it, but allowed his next tear to linger.

She brushed at her own tears. There were so many of them she stopped trying to contain them.

The room was filled with an undeniable happiness. Each of them, Alyssa and Joseph, couldn't contain themselves. The moment was without time, no hours, no minutes, no seconds. Their embrace was timeless.

"When?" Joseph asked.

"Seven months," she answered. "Oh, Joseph, I love you more than you will ever know. I worry about you, Joseph. I worry about you every time you fly. I've not told you that before. There are times when I sit and cry knowing you are in the air, depending on your skills, and that *Angel* of yours."

Her tears were washing over her face. She struggled to continue. "You must be safe, Joseph. I don't think I could live without you. I think of your father and your mother. I want a lifetime with you Joseph, not just four days like they had."

"Alyssa," he held her. "I'll be safe. You know I will. I didn't know it troubled you so. I'm so sorry."

She controlled her sobbing. “Even since you had the flame out over the North Sea; I’m terrified, Joseph. I’m sorry, but I am. And now, we have a beautiful gift from God. I couldn’t bear losing you.”

The minutes passed. Neither spoke.

Joseph brushed her face with his fingers. He looked at her, his love evident in his concern. He felt her fears and she could feel his love.

“I’m such a child,” she lamented. “I’ve ruined the happiest of surprises, haven’t I?”

“No,” he said holding her ever so tightly. “In fact, you gave me the best surprise of my life, but you also gave me a reminder of your undeniable love for me.”

She managed a smile. She kissed him and then ran her finger across his cheek. “Joseph, if only you knew how much I love you. If you only knew.”

Alyssa buried her head in his chest. Silence filled the room.

The letter in the baby carriage remained unopened. The shiny new Saint Christopher medal remained untouched as it gently swayed from the handle of the carriage.

* * * * *

Alyssa's search for Mark Dixon would be put on hold. What she would find, many years later, would renew her life.

JOSEPH AND MARGARET

FEBRUARY 1978
JOURNAL DISCUSSION

Joseph explained the wonderful memories shared by his mother and his father. The father he had not known. At times, tears welled in his eyes. His final comment to Margaret was, "Mum loved dad so much. I can't begin to understand her feelings."

Margaret nodded. She continued to be unsure of what Anne had written in her journal. Did she write the entire story or had she left one page of her life to be remembered by the memory of time. Margaret phrased the question carefully.

"Did your mother tell how thrilled she was the day you were born?"

Joseph smiled and opened the page of his mothers journal. "It's right here Margaret. I memorized the page number." He pointed to the sentence and read aloud. "I am blessed by my God. He has given me this wonderful gift."

Joseph pointed at the smudge of ink on the page. "I believe she must have cried when she wrote this next line."

Anne wrote, "Oh, Joseph, how I wish you could be here to see your son. He is everything you ever dreamed of."

Joseph wiped another tear from his eye. "I wish I would have known him, Margaret. He must have been a gentleman and he, at least to me, was a hero."

Margaret looked away for a brief moment. Silently she thanked Anne. Turning back to Joseph she took his hand and told him "Your mother was the finest woman I have ever known, Joseph. Your father was an absolute saint. Together they lived four days of the most complete love and understanding that the world has ever known. If either of them ever committed a wrong," she looked at Joseph with a tenderness Joseph had not seen in Margaret before that very moment, "then their wrong produced a gift that both of them would cherish for a lifetime."

Later, Joseph finished sharing the stories of Anne's journal and Joseph's diary. As he opened the door to leave, the sun had given way to the misty darkness of the London evening.

He walked to the bottom of the steps, turned and faced Margaret.

"It's not wrong to love someone, Margaret. What my mum and dad did was the most beautiful thing in the world. Love should never be buried under the burden of guilt. It should be valued and remembered and talked about so perhaps, in time, we will all feel the enormity of their feelings for each other."

He started to add something but thought better of it. Instead he waved and turned to walk away. The mist of the evening moistened his face. He turned one last time.

"Margaret," he beckoned, "thank you for being my mother's friend."

And then he was gone.

COLTISHALL

1982

ORDERS

The orders were short and to the point. The Coltishall air group would be one of several air units to be sent to the Falkland Islands. The pilots were given thirty-six hours to attend to personal business and say goodbye to loved ones.

* * * * *

For Joseph and Todd it was a heart wrenching time. Captain Todd Early and Denise spent the hours together at "Hadley House." The time together was like a blur. Both found it difficult to find proper words to express their feelings. Denise held Todd's hand, afraid to let go, for fear he would suddenly disappear. Despite their closeness the uncertainty of the days that were to follow seemed to claim their every word. The stately house remained ghostly quiet. No words seemed fitting for this woeful time.

Todd's parents remained in the background. Lord Early found it difficult to contain his emotions.

"You must leave them alone, Harold; you cannot begin to imagine what they are going through," Elizabeth remarked, "This is their time together. Put yourself in Denise's shoes will you. How on earth can the poor dear function?" She straightened the dust ruffle on the large davenport. "Her poor heart must be breaking."

"Oh for bloody sakes, Elizabeth, do you think for a moment I don't understand their feelings. I do for god's sake. You seem to forget I'm his father. My heart is breaking as well." Harold Early suddenly looked as though he had aged twenty years. "The bloody Argentines have lost their bloody minds."

Elizabeth began to cry. She sat in the overstuffed gray wingback chair that overlooked the stables. "Oh, Harold. Will it all end soon?"

He sat on the arm of the chair comforting her. He answered, "He's a grand pilot, dear. I venture to say he's the best. I'm thankful he has young Joseph. They'll watch over each other. You'll see, Elizabeth. They will watch over each other. You'll see. Joseph will be sure he returns. I have the utmost respect for Joseph and our son."

* * * * *

Todd set his bag near the heavy brown oak doors. Turning, he saw the three of them standing under a family photograph that hung above the white brick fireplace. Even the bright yellow and red flowers, neatly placed on the mantel, seemed somewhat colorless to him.

He hesitated before speaking. "Well, there it is. All packed and ready to go. Old Freddie is waiting at the car. He's always on time. Never a minute late. Quite a loyal chap, old Freddie." Todd forced a smile.

Todd's father took a step forward, and then taking Elizabeth's hand, they approached their son. Denise remained at the fireplace.

"Son, come safely home. We'll take care of Denise. No need to worry."

"Don't worry about her, son," Elizabeth added. "We'll keep her busy. We'll keep her mind off things." She choked with emotion.

"Well, father," Todd began. "We have taken a good number of years preparing for things like this. You mustn't fret. I'm quite confident we will make short work of this foolish nonsense."

"Gallant words, son. It's what I would expect you to say." Harold embraced his son and then in a low whisper, "God be with you. I will wait for your return. Now say goodbye to your mother." His voice grew lower with each word. He controlled the emotions that consumed his heart and his mind. His calmness masked the fear that consumed his thoughts.

Elizabeth kissed her son on the forehead. Her sadness would not allow her to speak. She turned, took the hand of her husband, and walked from the room. Awkwardly, Todd turned to Denise.

"Well, darling. We said it all last night." Todd walked toward her, as Denise remained frozen in place, unable to move.

"I love you, Denise."

The tears covered her face. The anguish of the possibility that he might not return left her with an unspeakable burden. Denise dreading this final goodbye, "You made me a promise, Todd. I expect you to keep it." It was all she could say.

Todd embraced her, "Have I ever broken a promise?" He kissed her neck, "Be brave, I'll be home before you know it."

He returned to the door. Their eyes met, for what seemed an eternity. He nodded and closed the door behind him.

She heard Freddie acknowledge his arrival. "Very well now, Todd. I'll take your bag. Sad day it is. I can feel it, I can. Careful now, watch the step. There you go."

As Todd's parents entered the room, her emotions could not be contained. Denise collapsed into Elizabeth's arms.

"Denise! My God Harold, call a doctor."

* * * * *

Joseph packed his kit. In between the quiet moments he found time to play with young Albert. The boy was almost four now. As energetic as a young tiger in the jungle.

"Sit here, next to me." Joseph took his son's hand.

"Where are you going, daddy?" The tone of the boy's words seemed to fit the occasion. He was sad, recognizing somewhere deep inside his young mind that this departure was different than all the others. "Will you be gone for a long time?"

"Well son, I expect that depends on a lot of people this time. Your father must follow orders, you know. Just as you must do what mother tells you, I must listen to my officers and if we do well I think they will allow us to return home. Sooner that you think."

Albert nodded his head. "Okay then, you tell those officers I want you to come home to be with mother and me." He contemplated his next words. "If you don't come home who will take care of mother?"

"Who said anything about not coming home?" Joseph asked.

"Jamie said you were going to fight a war and sometime people who fight wars don't come home. Is he telling the truth, father?"

Joseph tried his best to hide this from his son but young Jamie, Alyssa's nephew, had obviously taken liberty with the events unfolding in the South Atlantic.

"Well, Albert, if someone doesn't return home from a journey then guess what?"

"What?" Albert asked.

"Then mommies and little boys have to love each other forever. Little boys must grow up and be kind to mommy and take care of her. But I don't think you have to worry about such things."

"What does war mean?" His son's eyes seemed to demand an answer.

"Well, son," Joseph stopped and took his son in his arms. "War means . . ."

Alyssa walked into the room. She wore a blue skirt with a white blouse and a small gold necklace. She took Albert from Joseph and said, "War, son, is a bad thing. That's all you need to know. Now off with you and leave daddy and me alone for awhile." She kissed him, "Off with you, now!"

"Four years old and as inquisitive as a university student," Joseph offered.

"Too damn smart, if you ask me," Alyssa replied.

Joseph fastened the flaps on his kit. "Well that's it, I suppose. I always forget something. I wonder what it will be this time?"

"Oh dear Captain, you always forget me. Why is it you never find room in your kit for me? I'd cheer you when you needed it," she chided.

"I'm afraid if I packed you my sweetie, the Royal Air Force would lose a pilot. I would be forever grounded, looking forward to your delicious punishment."

"You have a dirty mind, Captain Howard. How dare you refer to my punishment as delicious? I must be more stern next time."

"I'll eagerly await my time in the clutches of my warden, then," he smiled.

Alyssa held him; they could feel the desire that had been evident from the day they first met.

"Oh, Joseph, I…" she stopped short of finishing.

"Say it," he prodded. "When you end a sentence in mid stream, I find it is always meant to be a profound statement befitting England's most beautiful barrister."

"You know me too well, my darling."

"Then go on. What words of enlightment and penetrating philosophy will grace my heart and mind?"

"I don't know if you want to hear them," she punched him lightly on the arm.

"What better time my sweetie? I'll soon be walking out the door, not knowing when I will return, and therefore I won't be able to debate your words of wisdom."

"Barristers love debate." She challenged, "Admit it Joseph. You're no match for me when it comes to a grand debate. Pilots are slow of wit and long on the art of making love."

"And what do you wish from me? The skill of Robertson or the adeptness and efficiency of Valentino?"

Alyssa laughed gleefully. "You sell yourself short, dear Captain. Valentino was no match for you."

"You flatter me."

"I love you," and with that the tears filled her eyes. "Joseph! Oh, Joseph!"

He held his wife as though it would be the last time. He held her tightly in his arms, not wanting to let go.

The minutes passed. The room remained silent. Alyssa didn't want the moment to end. She managed to ask him, between sobs, "You'll come back?"

He didn't answer. He continued to embrace her.

"Joseph," she asked again. "You will come home?"

Finally, not receiving an answer Alyssa buried her head in his chest. She wept uncontrollably. Her body wrenched in fear. "Answer me, Joseph. I need you to answer me. Lie if you have to, but I need you to answer me." She clenched her fist and hit him sternly on his chest; then her strength left her. "Joseph, please." Her tears covered his uniform.

"I'll come home, Alys. I'm sorry. I feel you next to me. I can feel your doubts and your alarm. I feel the uncertainty in your mind. For the first time, I understand what it must have been like for mother and father. What they must have endured and what mom lived with for all these years."

Joseph tightened his embrace. "I'll be home, Alyssa. Before you can realize it, I'll be home."

"Thank you Joseph. I need your reassurance. I need you. I can't exist without you. Oh Joseph, what would I do with Albert? I need you to raise him. I'm not like your mother. I couldn't go on without you.

"Shh!!" Joseph calmed her nerves. "Enough of what might be. No more worrying. Just the anticipation of my return. Do we have an agreement, or do I need some sort of legal document?" He did his best to relieve her fears.

"Make love to me Joseph. Please," she pleaded. "Make love to me."

"I must go, Alys. I'm late."

"I don't care how late you are. I don't care if they confine you to quarters and I don't care if *Angel* sits on the ground until she rusts away."

She cried again, "Make love to me Joseph!"

He closed the door. They made love through the tears and emotion. They made love as if it would be their last time.

THE DEPARTURE

1982
PORTSMOUTH, ENGLAND

HMS Hermes rested quietly near the now empty dock. Every conceivable supply had been loaded into the bowels of the ship. On deck, and below, were the Jaguars. They, too, seemed peaceful, betraying the turbulent task that lay before them.

Laced to the deck, forward of the other Jaguars, sat *Angel* and *Pepito*. Joseph made his way to *Angel*. He sat in the cockpit, taping a photograph of Alyssa and his son Albert, to the control console. When he completed the task he placed his finger on the image of Alyssa's face. In the photo, her hair was windblown across her face, her smile was inviting and alluring, and her eyes seemed to say, I love you. "And other things," he thought out loud

His son was laughing as though he had just witnessed a room full of clowns performing crazy antics that only a child would find humorous. The photograph was his favorite. The simple snapshot had caught them, as he wanted to remember them; happy, carefree, full of love and both as beautiful as ever.

Before climbing from *Angel*, Joseph reached for the token. As always it was attached to the air intake lever, quietly assuming it's role as protector of travelers. In this case the protector of *Angel* and himself. Saint Christopher was his loyal companion and on this mission he prayed Saint Christopher would provide him with a safe return to his wife and son.

"Hey," Todd yelled from the flight deck. "We have forty minutes before we cast off. C'mon, lets find a spot next to the starboard lines."

"I'm on my way. Hold on a minute," Joseph answered. He studied Alyssa's face. He could feel the emotion building in his mind. "Is this how you felt, father? With each passing event I believe I can understand your moments together." He paused again. "I've had so much more time with Alyssa. We've grown so close. And Albert, well, I know my son. We have shared so much time together. I guess I was just a wonderful dream to you. But, I do feel your presence. I always have, father, and I always will. Mom loved you. Oh, how she loved you. Until her last day, she worshiped your every move, your every smile. She said you were her knight in shining armor. I hope both of you are happy now. I know you waited a long time to share your life together."

"Hey, Joseph, c'mon old boy. We'll miss a good spot." Todd was growing impatient. "Let's go!"

"Be right there," Joseph, climbing from the cockpit, paused one more time. "Mom, I know now how you felt back then when you were young and innocent. So in love. I know mom because I believe Alyssa feels every emotion you experienced. Be with her mom. If somehow you can be with her I would be forever grateful."

He touched the photograph again. This time, however, his fingers were moist with his tears. Alyssa and Albert weighed on his heart and mind. He loved them more than they would ever know.

* * * * *

The HMS Hermes left Portsmouth on April 5, 1982. She rendezvoused with the fleet, eleven destroyers and a frigate. There were three submarines and an assault ship. In the end over one hundred ships and 25,000 men would take part in the war. On this cloudy, overcast, and rainy day the Portsmouth fleet set sail for the Falkland Islands. The weather was fitting for the occasion. Despite the ordeal that lay ahead there was an excitement on board. An excitement that filled the very soul of warriors as they prepared for combat.

There is something strange about this excitement. It is part glory and part patriotic. It is a duty that must be fulfilled. And yet at the first taste of war, the excitement fades and it gives way to fear and the never ending will to survive. From the time the first combat takes place a man fights, not for glory or flag, but he fights to return home, to the family he loves.

* * * * *

The fleet refueled at the US base on the Ascension Island. Joseph watched as England's unwavering ally provided the lifeblood to allow them to continue their journey. As he silently watched the American ships transfer oil and fuel a thought crossed his mind.

"It's happening all over again. England and America."

A strange feeling invaded his mind. He shuddered and felt an ominous fear. Uneasiness consumed his thoughts. Later he dreamed of aircraft exploding in the sky, and oddly enough, he dreamed of peace and serenity.

THE FALKLAND WAR

1982

FALKLAND ISLANDS

SOUTH ATLANTIC

The Argentine, French built, Mirage Fighter exploded in mid air. *Pepito*, Todd's Jaguar, climbed steadily through the smoke and debris.

"Ah," the radio cracked with static. "Nice going Todd." Joseph was closing on his wing.

"Oh, Oh!" Todd pointed forward. Two sleek Mirage Fighters were closing fast.

"I'll take the one on the right. The other is yours," Joseph broke off; a Mirage broke with him. Todd headed straight for his target. *Pepito* and the remaining Mirage would soon be in firing range. Todd's radar locked on his target.

Joseph read the data being fed into his computer display. His over wing sidewinder infrared missiles were still intact. His two Aden 30mm cannons were at his disposal, but for this Mirage, he would use the sidewinder.

His computer locked on the Argentine fighter. He released the missile. Within seconds the Mirage exploded, wings and fuselage falling into the waters of the Atlantic.

Speeding past the spot where the Mirage had been, his Angel, the Jaguar GR1B with the long sleek fuselage and large swept tail fins and rudder raced to find Todd. The relatively short-span swept wings continued to carry a potent punch. Two sidewinders remained at his disposal.

"Joseph," the voice seemed distressed.

"Todd. I'm okay. I'm on my way."

"Hurry old chap. I've got my bloody hands full over here."

"I see you now." Joseph bore down on one of the two Argentine planes that trailed Todd.

Unknowingly, and as a force of habit, he whispered to himself, "I am the angel of death. I come from the skies, unannounced . . ."

Before he could finish, his two 30mm Aden cannons let loose a deadly stream of fire. Joseph continued to fire until he saw smoke emerging from the Mirage. The Argentine broke away, leaving one Argentine fighter engaged with Todd's Jaguar, *Pepito*.

Banking sharply, Joseph closed again. His air speed reached nine hundred ten miles per hour. He gave *Angels* Turbo Meca/Rolls Royce Adour turbo fans full power. His Saint Christopher medal was shaking violently.

"Ah, bloody hell," Todd barked into the radio. "I damn well have an Exocet missile closing on me," Todd dove for the ocean. *Pepito* strained for speed. In a matter of seconds the Exocet would blow him to pieces. The missile closed on *Pepito*. Todd realized that he no longer could outrun the speeding missile.

"Joey, I think . . ."

Captain Todd Early heard the explosion. He strained to see behind him. All he could see was an empty sky.

"Joseph, what the bloody hell happened?"

ALYSSA HOWARD AND SERGEANT MARK DIXON

MAY 3, 2000

BEAUFORT, SOUTH CAROLINA USA

Marvin Kessler, her driver, politely opened Alyssa's door. Kessler was dressed in his usual black suit, white shirt, and black tie. The clothing was dated and showed signs of wear; the pocket and lapel of his suit coat was frayed from years of dedicated service to his loyal customers. One cuff of his tattered and worn chauffeurs trousers hung loosely over his venerable black shoes. Even his one remaining white limousine was beginning to show signs of age as a few rust spots appeared near the trunk and underneath the passenger doors.

What didn't show wear and tear was Mr. Kessler's pleasing personality. Despite several years of retirement as the owner of a limousine service, the seventy-one year old southern gentlemen, was doing Mark Dixon a favor. A favor that Kessler wanted to provide to Dixon for years, but Dixon, in his usual manner, had always refused.

Dixon, for as long as Kessler could remember, serviced his fleet of limousines that provided service to low country citizens during occasions such as weddings, parties, or trips to the airport. His limousines, at one time or another, provided transportation for movie stars, politicians, and dignitaries from foreign countries. Dixon kept Kessler's fleet in tiptop shape, often performing repairs at no charge. Kessler knew this, but Dixon shrugged it off, offering as an excuse, Kessler's charitable works for needy children.

Through the years the two of them had become inseparable friends, sharing stories, fishing, taking care of each other and sharing their unselfish honesty with the people of Beaufort. There was something about Kessler that provided Alyssa with an immediate impression. There was an aged dignity about the man. His character was beyond reproach and he, despite his age, was poised and he had this incredible humbling grace about him. She was soon to learn that Sergeant Dixon had the same qualities as well as a majestic nobleness that was evident in his every word and deed.

"Ma'am," Kessler offered as he opened Alyssa's door. "This here is the home of Mark Dixon." He paused for a moment as he assisted Alyssa from the limousine. "Of course, to you, Sergeant Dixon, Ma'am. You can see he takes care of things here. He'd put on some years, ninety in fact, but he still finds time to work in his flowers. Beautiful," he pointed to a small garden near an aged oak tree. "Yes sir ree. He loves his flowers."

"They are beautiful," Alyssa remarked. "In fact quite remarkable. So many bright and vivid colors. Why I'd swear it was an English garden." Alyssa walked to the patch of color. Kessler followed her. Alyssa's flowered print dress seemed an appropriate choice for this charming and radiant southern setting.

"Oh! They are beautiful," she knelt before a miniature pink rose bush and smelled the delightful fragrance. "He takes care of this by himself, you say?"

"Yes Ma'am, he does." Kessler shook his head slowly. "I'm afraid it's all he does these days. He's up in age now, Ms. Howard. Has all he can do to get around, but he has this pride about him." Kessler shuffled his worn black shoes on the dark green Bermuda grass. "As I told you earlier, he is a spiritual man. A man of great conviction; honest as the day is long." Then he added, "He said the day this old oak tree dies will be the day he goes home to his Lord." He pointed to the oak; it's leaves providing shade as it had for over one hundred years. "I'm afraid this ancient tree will be around for many years after Sergeant Dixon is gone. It's as healthy as all get out. Never loses a leaf until the fall weather takes its toll."

Suddenly, without warning, two Marine fighters from the Beaufort Marine Air Station interrupted their conversation. The fighters, gray in color, were at treetop level, flying in perfect formation. Their wingtips were as close as one could imagine. As they passed, the roar of jet engines shook the sky. The earth trembled under Alyssa's feet. Her imagination produced a vision of *Pepito* and *Angel*, side by side, as they had flown many years earlier.

Without giving it a thought, she instinctively raised her hand–and waved at the invisible Marine pilots. She stood, looking through the green trees, until the sound of freedom succumbed to the distance between her and the heavens.

Gaining her composure, she stood, then looked at her chauffeur. She knew Sergeant Dixon had graciously offered Mr. Kessler's services. She offered to pay him, but Kessler said it was out of the question. He shook his head and replied, "No Ma'am. I have often asked your friend to provide him with a favor and now after all these years, you, Ms. Howard, have finally given me the last opportunity to receive my wish. No Ma'am, I couldn't accept your generosity but you must accept his, Sergeant Dixon's. He's waited for this day for a long long time. He's waited for you, Ms. Howard. He knew you would come. He told me that one day you or a woman named Anne Howard would come by. You know, visit him is what he meant." She remembered how Kessler seemed to look off into the distance before continuing; "He swore God would bring you here. Often said when that happened his life would be complete. I hope that doesn't mean. . ." Kessler stopped, looked at Alyssa with a knowing gloom in his eyes, and turned away as if to examine the primitive marshlands surrounding Dixon's home.

Now she was here. In Sergeant Dixon's yard waiting to meet the man who perhaps held the answers to her questions about a B-17 named *Angel*, her crew, and her mother-in-law, Anne Howard. Perhaps, she thought, even answers about her husband.

* * * * *

"Ma'am, I believe we should see him now." Kessler waved his hand in a southern gesture, motioning to the well kept home surrounded by stately trees and well manicured lawns.

"Yes, by all means. I didn't mean to dally here. It's all so charming." She followed him up the brick path to the front door. "Mr. Kessler," she beckoned her driver.

"Yes, Ms. Howard?"

"One more question please?" She pointed towards the ancient oak, "The white stringy matter hanging from the tree. What's it called?"

"Oh, the moss," Kessler responded with a smile. "It is called Spanish moss, Ma'am. Been around South Carolina since the beginning of time. It's our southern trademark, Ms. Howard. South Carolina wouldn't be South Carolina without Spanish moss.

"So the Spanish moss has been hanging on to Sergeant Dixon's tree for all those years?"

"I would venture to say, Ma'am. And it will be there for years to come. It's our heritage Ms.; it sure is."

Alyssa admired the moss. Her eyes remained fixed on the tree and it's ancient accessory. She felt as though the tree was somehow speaking to her.

Then, without warning, a gentle breeze began to blow across the low country. The soft wind came so suddenly that both she and Mr. Kessler were taken by its presence. There was a strange coolness to it. Almost mystical.

Both she and Mr. Kessler stared at the elderly and patriarchal oak tree. Its dark green leaves began to fall, slowly at first, and then more rapidly. A large clump of moss rocked to and fro and then fell to the ground.

"What's happening?" Alyssa turned to Kessler, "What's happening?" An urgency claimed her voice.

A tear seemed to be visible in the driver's eye. "Ma'am, I think you better hurry. He's waited a long time."

"It can't be. No!" Alyssa trembled. Emotions overcame her. "This can't be happening."

"Please Ms. Howard. Please, hurry. He's waited..."

* * * * *

Dixon sat in his overstuffed chair. When they entered the room a slow, easy smile crossed his face. He started to rise but his friend, Kessler moved toward him.

"That'll be okay, Sergeant. You just stay right where you are. No need to get up."

Kessler placed his hand on Dixon's arm, but before he could introduce Alyssa Howard to him, Dixon offered, "You must be Ms. Howard?"

Alyssa moved across the large living room with its many windows that provided a breath taking view of the green marshlands. The sight was impressive and captivating.

"Sergeant Dixon," she took his outstretched hand in hers. "I've waited so long to meet you. It's such an honor and privilege to be here." Alyssa examined his features. "You are so kind to see me."

Dixon squeezed her hand as best he could. "I too, have waited for this day. Since 1944, I've waited for you or Anne–Anne Howard–to come here. And now, well here we are. Just as I imagined it." He was dressed in dark brown khakis and an oversized tan khaki shirt. His eyes seemed to strain as he examined this proper English woman standing before him.

He looked to his friend. "Ms. Howard must be thirsty. I have some refreshments in the icebox, for both of you. Could you. . . ?"

"I will," Kessler replied.

"It's not necessary," Alyssa looked at Kessler and then to Dixon.

"Heaven, Ma'am. You haven't lived until you taste the Sergeants famous watermelon lemonade. Why everyone in Beaufort swears it is the best warm weather refresher in all of South Carolina."

Kessler gave Alyssa a look of concern. His eyes seemed alarmed as he turned away.

"Excuse me, please. I'll just help your friend carry the glasses. I'm anxious to try this famous drink of yours." Alyssa followed Kessler to the kitchen.

"What is it? You look–please," she pleaded, "tell me this isn't happening."

Before she could finish Kessler whispered, "Ma'am, I'll get the refreshments." He took her hand, "You go in and talk to him. Talk slowly. He has a difficult time hearing at times. Please, Ms. Howard."

As she returned to the living room, Mr. Kessler looked through the large kitchen window; the leaves were falling faster now. He noticed an alligator had suddenly appeared under the tree, his lazy and ancient eyes fixed on the house. He seemed to be waiting. Waiting for a promised event that even this creature of the wild seemed to understand.

Alyssa pulled a chair next to Dixon. "Sergeant Dixon, I have wondered for years about the mysteries surrounding *Angel*. The locket, Joseph Doglio, and in fact the whole story. I'm wondering if you can shed some light on the stories and perhaps set my mind at ease. I don't know where to begin and I'm afraid I feel so unworthy of your presence."

Dixon took her hand in his. His hand was unstable and it seemed to shake uncontrollably.

Now, while speaking, his voice was transformed. It suddenly appeared strong as a youthful energy claimed his mind. Sergeant Dixon came to life; his determined and powerful voice filled the room.

"Ms. Howard, we must begin at the beginning," he smiled. "The day of the *Angel* crews first mission. You see it was that mission that defined God's presence and the message He intended to leave behind by giving those of us who were surrounded by pain and grief a reason to believe; to believe in His promise and in His grace. The story begins with a tear and in reality, for me, it never ended. You see, Ms. Howard, His promises have no ending. Only hope."

"Now my dear, the tear. Let me tell you my experience with the tear. That mysterious tear blest *Angel's* face and later that same tear blest my life. It still does."

Dixon was alive now. Each story took on a new meaning. Each story was a vivid reminder of his life and the life of so many kind and spiritual friends.

He told Alyssa of the tear, the spiritual messages inside the flying Fortress named *Angel* and he told her of the last mission of the crew. "You've been a good friend," Hawkins told him. Did Hawkins know? He spoke of O'Neill and his sudden conversion, the diary of Second Lieutenant Joseph Doglio, and of course, the locket.

Occasionally a tear would fall from his eye. The tear would catch in a crevice under his eye, only to move slowly down his face, as another tear would gently speed its progress.

The play book, the window, the roses placed in Mrs. Doglio's car, and there was the dream of the nurse that lovingly took care of Mrs. Hawkins.

Alyssa was taken by Sergeant Dixon's story of 398th member, Lieutenant Harbaugh, who witnessed the crew forty years after their demise. Lieutenant Harbaugh saw a Saint Christopher medal in the sand but when he tried to reach for it, the token disappeared, as did the eight crewmen who beckoned him to the island located on a lake in Cashiers, North Carolina.

Alyssa was mesmerized by the accounts of days gone by. Some accounts, five decades past, others that took place only months earlier. As she listened, peacefulness filled her heart. A strange and sudden understanding filled her very soul.

"My husband nearly lost his life over the North Sea." Alyssa explained the day in May 1977 when Joseph's *Angel*, the Royal Air Force Jaguar, lost power.

"Lieutenant Doglio swore, after his *Angel* made it across the North Sea," Dixon paused, 'that the North Sea would never claim the life of a Doglio. He kept his promise Ms. Howard. By the grace of God, he kept his promise.'

Tears filled Alyssa eyes. She took his hand and held it tightly. "I understand now. After all these years, it's all so clear to me. I don't know what to say."

Dixon pulled her toward him. She placed her head on his chest. Her sobbing seemed to give her an inner peace.

Kessler, in the kitchen, continued to stare out the window. In a matter of a few hours, the ancient oak had lost its leaves. Only a few remained, waiting for the final genteel southern breeze to claim their last moment of glory. He noticed the alligator had slowly made its way to the marsh, now filled with water, as high tide had emerged on the reeds and willows of the beautiful low country. The alligator looked back, for one last time, and then disappeared into the reeds.

Kessler moved to the door. He watched as Dixon, Sergeant Dixon, held Alyssa in his arms.

Kessler strained to hear as the once proud Sergeant uttered his last words. His voice had lost its strength. The words were barely audible but there was a peacefulness about them; a final peacefulness that seemed to envelope the room.

"Ms. Howard, you must remember that God provided gifts and God forgives. He provides gifts that are sometimes taken from us and He returns those gifts when it is His will to do so. You may find it difficult to believe but Mr. Kessler, there," he pointed to the doorway, "he's been an angel to me for a good many years. We all have angels. We just don't admit it. But angels have blest you, dear Alyssa, and now you have become an angel to me. Life goes full circle you see."

Alyssa could feel him weakening. It was happening so quickly.

"Ms. Howard," he whispered. His every word was strained, life leaving him as though his last wish had been granted. "It's time for me and my oak tree to go now."
Sergeant Dixon smiled and motioned Kessler to come near him.

"Kessler, dear friend, would you do me one more favor? After all these years I seem to be asking for all my favors in one day."

Kessler, shaking with age, nodded, "What is it you would like me to do, my friend?"

Dixon smiled and replied, "Please call my daughter. She would want to be here, with Ms. Howard and me.

Tell her I'll wait, but tell her not to take long." His voice wavered and seemed to crack with emotion. The kind of emotion that years of love produces between father and daughter.

His daughter pulled into the long driveway. She drove as fast as she could. Her emotions conjured her every thought. She ran across her fathers lawn, not bothering to close the door of her gray station wagon.

She opened the door to her father's home. Two minutes later the last leaf fell from the majestic oak tree, slowly floating to the South Carolina lowlands. A gentle breeze lifted the leaf until in landed on his colorful flower garden. The leaf lingered and then blew across the lawn and into the watery marsh.

The leaf skimmed the rising water until it gently came to rest near a weary eyed alligator who slowly and sadly made his way to where all alligators go to find peace and rest. He didn't look back. He knew his friend had left him and now he would search in an unknown and strange place for the man named Sergeant Mark Dixon. He disappeared from view at the same moment that Alyssa placed her hand on the brooding oak tree.

"I believe, Joseph. I believe." Her tears comforted her.

The wind raised her words above the marshland. She knew Joseph would hear them. The words faded into the clouds and drifted through the heavens.

* * * * *

Two men and a woman sat under an aged B-17 Flying Fortress. The smiling face of an angel adorned the fuselage of the aircraft. They didn't speak as they heard the words slowly enter the heavens.

They stood, walking to a group of men smartly dressed in World War II uniforms. Young Joseph paused to listen -- the word fell quietly on his ear.

BELIEVE

Second Lieutenant Joseph Doglio turned toward Anne, he took her hand and said, "I'd like you to meet an old friend. . ."

EPILOGUE

Captain Joseph Earl Howard lost his life during the Falkland Island War. He was killed on May 18, 1982. Eyewitness accounts indicate Captain Howard maneuvered his Jaguar, named *Angel*, into the path of an Argentine Exocet missile. His actions saved the life of his best friend, Captain Todd Early.

* * * * *

Alyssa Howard, now fifty-six years old, lives in Edinborough, Scotland. She was devastated by the lost of her husband. She raised their son, as did Anne Howard, with love, patience and understanding. Alyssa continuously, through the years, told her son, the stories of his father and of his grandmother and grandfather. She vowed to keep their memory alive. She challenged her son to do the same.

Alyssa Howard, during the year 2000, renewed her search for Sergeant Mark Dixon. To her surprise, she found him, and during their visit her life was forever changed. Her faith restored.

* * * * *

Albert Joseph Howard is now a Captain in the Royal Air Force. His devotion to his mother grows with each passing day. Attached to the canopy lever in his Harrier Aircraft is an aged Saint Christopher medal. The token, as was the case with his father and grandfather, is his constant companion.

* * * * *

Sergeant Mark Dixon, the crew chief, for a World War II, B-17g named *Angel*, lived in Beaufort, South Carolina. He was ninety years old when he passed away. Dixon attended church every Sunday morning as well as the mid-week service on Wednesday evening. As he grew older, his hands no longer functioned the way they did many years ago. They showed signs of years of hard work, almost totally paralyzed, and the oil and grease imbedded in his fingers was a part of his legacy. Dixon continued to swear he heard *Angel* flying across the lowland areas of Beaufort County. His claims were justified when, on one foggy morning, he and his granddaughter heard the engines of a B-17. Rushing to the door to witness the sound, he found, on his door, an old photograph of a blue sky and the words, "I'm trying," were written across the face of the picture. It was the same picture that Carroll O'Neill had taped near his tail gun position during World War II. He prayed again, knowing his willingness to "Believe" in the miracle of miracles had been rewarded.

* * * * *

Captain Todd Early retired from the Royal Air Force in 1987. He and his wife, Denise, reside at "Hadley House." His parents have both passed away. He has a son, Joseph Todd Early, and a daughter, Anne Elizabeth Early. Captain Early set aside a trust fund for his friend's son. The fund allowed young Joseph to attend a university and he, in turn, graduated with honors. Although Alyssa was reluctant to accept the gift she did so to benefit her son. She was not told who administered the fund but surmised it was a gift from Captain Early. Captain Early was honored on March 5, 1996 for his charitable work. His contributions and dedicated service to charitable organizations were graciously provided in memory of Captain Joseph Earl Howard, his dearest friend.

* * * * *

Second Lieutenant Joseph Doglio, the navigator of *Angel*, is buried in the Braceville-Gardner Illinois Cemetery. His remains rest quietly alongside his parents. Each year, on July 19, a bouquet of flowers is mysteriously placed on his grave. The flowers are simple. Attached to the flowers is a card that simply says, “I will always love you.”

* * * * *

Anne Howard succumbed to cancer in 1977. Her friend, Margaret Crueller, asked that a lovely, but aged, gold locket be placed in her casket at the time of her burial. This request was granted. The locket was attached to the sleeve of her dress. The morning of her burial, while paying last respects, Margaret was taken back by what she saw. The locket was no longer attached to Anne’s sleeve, but neatly placed around her neck. Upon questioning, Mr. Peeve, the undertaker, denied moving the locket and declared that it was impossible for it to have been moved at all as the casket is closed at night and the doors of his establishment are locked and secured. Margaret smiled and calmly remarked, "Not to worry Mr. Peeve. It's where she would have wanted it to be."

* * * * *

Margaret Crueller's loyal friendship for Anne now spans almost six decades. Now eighty years of age, Margaret visits the graves of Anne and Captain Joseph Earl Howard on a weekly basis. She has been a source of encouragement for Alyssa and her son. She refuses to discuss Second Lieutenant Earl Hart, because she says, his memories belong to her. Those wonderful and most marvelous moments will remain with her until she is called home.

* * * * *

The mysteries are much discussed. One can find explanations for these extraordinary events but if one is a barrister, then one must admit there are only a few hard facts to prove or disprove any of the events that occurred to the crew of *Angel* or to their families. One can only have faith that miracles do exist and the miracles that surrounded the *Angel* crew, Anne Howard, and their families are a message to all of us.

Mark Dixon, the spiritual man from Beaufort, South Carolina, when asked if the stories in his mind are indeed true, answered by looking me straight in the eye. He smiled, shook his head in an all knowing way. Then he said one word. The word will remain with me all the days of my life... "BELIEVE"

THE MIRROR OF TIME

PRESENT DAY
JOSEPH AND HENRY

Second Lieutenant Joseph Doglio was sixteen years old when I was born. Four years later, on November 2, 1942, Joseph enlisted in the United States Army Air Force. I don't remember Joseph although I am certain that there was a time when he stood over my crib and with his hand he gently touched my head. I have no doubt he smiled at his newly born cousin. Such were family ties in South Wilmington, Illinois, a town of six-hundred people.

I often wonder about Joseph's personality. The people I interviewed told me he was an extraordinary young man. Kind, religious, and happy go lucky. People were quick to add that he never met a stranger.

Oh, the list of descriptive words go on and on. But from my conversations I quickly drew a mental image of Joseph. As days past, and chapters of this book were completed,

I became ever more aware of Joseph mannerisms. At times I swear I actually felt his presence.

Occasionally I would talk with people, friends and strangers, and I would try to match their personalities and mannerisms to what I envisioned Joseph to be.

There were times when a few of my images of Joseph would fit well with a particular person. But, a few, or several, were not enough to say, "That's the person who best fits my mental image of the cousin I never knew." The kind and gentle war hero who became the subject of three short stories detailing his life, his love, his kindness, and his gentle way with strangers.

Then, in the summer of 2001, I was suddenly introduced to the one man who is everything Joseph was and would have been.

His friendship was immediate. His kindness was evident. His love for people is visible in all he does and in all he shares. His open arms and peaceful mannerisms portray his sense of values and honesty.

I haven't met his wife nor have I met his family. Someday I will. And when I do I'll tell them that my friend Henry Ristic reminds me of someone special.

I have no doubt they will answer by saying, "Our Henry IS special."

And I will nod and say to myself, "Yes, he is special. Just like Joseph would have been."

* * * * *

I don't know why I wrote this. Something or somebody made me realize it was necessary to tell you this. I don't question these feelings anymore. I just believe these extraordinary feelings are with me for a reason and for a purpose.

Second Lieutenant Joseph Doglio
Training 1943

Second Lieutenant Joseph Doglio

An *Angel* Falls From The Sky

The *Angel* Crashes

Germans Inspect Tail Section of *Angel*
July 1944

Colonel Harold Weekley And Author Don Gaddo
July 2001

To order additional copies of **War's Lost Love Found**, complete the information below.

Ship to: (please print)

Name______________________________

Address____________________________

City, State, Zip_______________________

Day phone__________________________

______copies of **War's Lost Love Found**

@ $20.00 each $________

Postage and handling @3.50 per book $________

NC residents add $1.30 tax $________

Total amount enclosed $________

Make checks payable to **Palmaya Publishing**

Send to: Don Gaddo
P.O. Box 773 • Chapel Hill, NC 27514

To order additional copies of **War's Lost Love Found**, complete the information below.

Ship to: (please print)

Name______________________________

Address____________________________

City, State, Zip_______________________

Day phone__________________________

______copies of **War's Lost Love Found**

@ $20.00 each $________

Postage and handling @3.50 per book $________

NC residents add $1.30 tax $________

Total amount enclosed $________

Make checks payable to **Palmaya Publishing**

Send to: Don Gaddo
P.O. Box 773 • Chapel Hill, NC 27514